JAMESON

A Brothers Ink Story

By
Nicole James

JAMESON

Brothers Ink
Book 1

By
Nicole James

Published by Nicole James
Copyright 2016 Nicole James
All Rights Reserved
Cover Art by Viola Estrella
Photography by Lane Dorsey
Model: Josh Mario John
ISBN#: 9781536897456

PROLOGUE

Jameson made his way down Main Street in Grand Junction, Colorado. It was a warm summer day. He paused on the corner, waiting for the light to change. His eyes skated over the postings on a pole, landing on one flyer in particular.

He did a double take.

What the hell?

He yanked it off the pole, his eyes scanning the details, and then he strode angrily down the street.

CHAPTER ONE

One week earlier—

A magazine was slapped down on the desk.

"That's who we need for the gala. Grand Junction's new golden boy."

Ava Hightower's eyes scanned the photo, and then flashed up to her assistant. As helpful as Stephanie was trying to be, there was no way *in hell* that was happening.

"You're joking, right?"

"Joking? Uh, *no*. Look at the man. He's gorgeous."

Ava's eyes again took in this month's issue of *Colorado Life Magazine*'s cover boy. Jameson O'Rourke: owner of *Brothers Ink*, the tattoo shop that had become the bane of her existence.

The photo was of him in a chair, the back twisted around so that he straddled it, his crossed, full-sleeved arms resting on the curved wood. The colorful ink ran up both forearms, silver rings on his hands, his blond hair long, and his eyes a vibrant blue, staring straight into the camera.

Straight into her soul, it seemed.

Now where had that thought come from?

She swallowed. Okay, she could admit he had his appeal—for a certain type of woman she supposed. But that certainly wasn't her. Not by a long shot.

She was a businesswoman who owned a prosperous employment agency specializing in temporary positions. She'd worked hard to make Hightower Staffing a success. She was also on the city council, a recent position that had put her butting heads with the arrogant Mr. O'Rourke at her very first meeting.

He'd tried to pass a resolution to obtain designated motorcycle parking for several spots in front of his business. She'd made sure the resolution was defeated and, in the process, made a permanent enemy of the newly crowned "King of Ink."

She dropped her head. Why, oh why had she chosen that to be her first battle? The man was the town's new hero. A rising superstar in the tattoo world, he'd been on the cover of several national magazines and even had a reality show about his shop and work.

She'd heard they'd followed him on his annual mecca to Sturgis last summer and filmed him. She'd also heard it had only lasted one season, probably because he was impossible. At least, that's the first impression she'd formed of the man.

She could still remember how he'd looked at her from across the room when she'd protested his plan to claim the three spots in front of his store. Like he had a right to three spots for goodness sake. She could only imagine the domino effect that would have had—every business in town would want their own designated spots and that would be a nightmare. Not to mention it flew in the face of her sense of freedom and fair play. Citizens should have the right to park in any public spot on Main Street. No one should be able to "lay claim" to any of them.

Stephanie—her assistant and sister—of course didn't know about her interaction with Mr. O'Rourke.

"We need a draw, Ava. A big one. If you could get Grand Junction's most eligible bachelor for the auction, we'd sell out. Guaranteed. It would be the most successful gala we've ever had. Hell, women would drive from miles around for this. And you wouldn't have to worry about it being in the red like last year."

Last year. As if Ava needed a reminder of what a fiasco that had been. They'd barely sold any tickets, and the donations had been dismal. The charity was so worthy and dear to her heart, she not only felt like she'd let herself down, but the charity *and* her late youngest sister.

Ava shoved the magazine back at Stephanie. "He'd never do it."

"Why do you say that? You haven't asked him."

"And I'm not going to."

"But why?"

"Never mind why."

"The gala would sell out. You know it would. If we had him, you wouldn't have to worry for the next couple of months. The tickets would sell themselves. You have to do it, Ava. We've rented the ballroom and everything. If we can't sell tickets again this year…"

Ava rubbed her forehead, feeling the beginnings of a headache coming on. "All right. I'll talk to him if I get a chance."

"If you get a chance? The flyers go to the printer tomorrow. And you're leaving town for that conference. You need to talk to him a.s.a.p."

"I said I'd do it, Steffy. Now leave me alone so I can make these calls, please."

Stephanie threw her hands up. "Fine. I'll go rework the flyer with his name and picture."

"Don't you dare! He hasn't agreed to participate yet."

"He will. It's for a good cause. How can he refuse?" Stephanie tossed over her shoulder as she exited.

Ava stared down at the cover and muttered, "Easily."

***

Ava was grabbing up her bag and heading out the door when Stephanie's voice had her stopping in her tracks.

"Don't forget to stop by Brothers Ink on your way to the airport."

"I know, Steffy. I'll give him the pitch, but I doubt he's going to do it."

"Of course he will."

Ava rolled her eyes and hurried out the door, Stephanie's words ringing in her ear.

She drove the couple of blocks to Brothers Ink, and after parking three spots down, she looked up at the building. She had to give the man credit. As tattoo shops went, it was an upscale place—more on the side of art gallery than seedy storefront.

As she sat in her car, she heard the roar of engines and saw several motorcycles pull up and back into a spot, their rear tires to the curb. The leather-clad men dismounted and headed inside the shop.

That sealed the deal *and* gave her the excuse she

needed to abandon this ridiculous idea in the first place. There was no way in hell she was walking in there now. Not with a bunch of scary bikers inside. She backed out and pulled away, heading toward the airport. Stephanie would just have to get over it. She'd tell her the man turned her down; which probably would have been the case anyway.

Maybe if she was lucky, she could silence her phone and tell Stephanie she'd had no signal at the airport. Then she could deal with Stephanie's disappointment next week when she returned. By then the flyers would have had to go to the printer to meet the Friday deadline, and Stephanie would have to take the mockup they'd already designed.

The Bachelor Auction's headlining bachelor will just have to be Dr. Ashton again, the bald plastic surgeon with the overbite. *Oh God, they'd never sell tickets.*

***

Stephanie finished up her work and shut down her computer. As she was gathering up her purse and things, she noticed the release form sitting on Ava's desk—the one she was supposed to have Jameson O'Rourke sign when she'd talked to him. *Damn it.* Without the signed consent, they couldn't get him in the flyer that had to be to the printer by 2:00 p.m.

tomorrow. If Jameson was their headliner, he needed to be in all the promotional materials.

She blew out a breath. She'd just have to run by his shop and get his signature herself. Glancing at her watch, she figured she had just enough time to stop by there before she had to be across town.

***

Stephanie entered the shop, a bell tinkling above her and drawing the attention of one of the tattoo artists who was bent over a customer at the moment.

"Be with you in a second, darlin'." He returned to his work, and she took the time to look around, her eyes going to the art on the walls and then to the larger wall displaying photographs of some of the artists' tattoos. The work was stunning. The colors vivid, the designs amazing, and they all reflected the renowned talent the shop had become known for.

Stephanie bit her lip, studying them. She'd thought more than once about getting a tattoo herself, but she'd never been able to decide on what.

"What can I do for you, pretty lady?"

She turned to find a man at the counter, his palms resting on the top. He was a big man with muscular arms, his tattoos revealed by a tight, short-sleeved shirt that strained over his pecs.

He had the prettiest brown eyes and a killer smile hiding behind several days' growth of dark beard. His hair was shorn close to his skull, and the look worked for him. *Really* worked for him.

She couldn't help but return his smile as she turned from the wall of art.

His eyes followed where she'd been looking.

"See something you like? I'd be glad to do the work myself."

She grinned. "Maybe someday."

His smile widened. "No time like the present, angel."

She watched as he leaned on his elbows, bringing him closer to her.

"I, um, I just needed to drop this release off for Mr. O'Rourke to sign."

He took the document, his eyes scanning over it. "There are four Mr. O'Rourke's here. Which one are you after? Please say it's me." His eyes met hers as he gave her that killer smile again.

She grinned in return. "Sorry. I'm looking for Jameson O'Rourke."

He nodded. "Why am I not surprised?" He scanned the document again. "What is this release for?"

"The charity gala. My boss stopped by earlier and

talked to him about it. She forgot this." She nodded to the form he held. "It's the release he needs to sign for us to put him in the promotional material as our headlining bachelor."

"Headlining bachelor?"

"It's an auction."

His grin got even bigger. "You sayin' you're going to auction off Jameson?"

"Well, for a date. It's all in fun and for a good cause. It's a black tie affair. Very respectable."

"I see. So, you're sayin' women are gonna bid on him?"

"That's the idea. The money we raise all goes to the charity."

"He gotta stand up on a stage for this, like some kind of beauty pageant contestant?"

"Um, yes, something like that."

"Just tell me one thing. There gonna be a runway he's gotta walk down?"

"Well, yes, actually there is."

He started laughing.

She frowned. "Is something funny? Do you think raising money for a charity is a big joke?"

He immediately tried to squelch his laughter. "No, ma'am, not at all. I'm sure Jameson would love to help out."

"Could you just see that he gets it? The flyers have to go to the printer by 2:00 p.m. tomorrow so the sooner I can get that back, the better."

"Where we gotta drop this off?"

"I can come back and pick it up."

"Oh no, no. I'll make sure we bring it by tomorrow morning."

"Okay." She pulled a card out of her purse and handed it to him. "Here's the address. Hightower Staffing Services."

He glanced at it, and she noted the grin that formed on his face when he saw her name on the card. "What time do you open up, Stephanie?"

"Nine."

"I'll deliver it personally."

She smiled. "Thank you."

"Sure I can't interest you in a tattoo?"

"Maybe next time."

He nodded. "See you tomorrow, then."

CHAPTER TWO

Ava set her purse and briefcase down on her desk. She was exhausted from her trip. The conference had been educational, but she was glad to be back. She was a bit of a control freak and hated to be away from the office, especially for an entire week.

Her eyes fell on the brightly colored flyer they'd designed for the charity gala, and her mouth fell open. She picked it up, studying it. *Dear God*, this had better be a joke.

There was a picture of Jameson O'Rourke, and in big block letters it proclaimed him the headlining bachelor for the auction.

"Stephanie!"

Her sister stuck her head around the doorframe. "How was your trip?"

"Never mind that. What is *this*?" She held up the paper.

"Our flyer. Great, huh?"

"Please tell me this is just a mockup. Please tell me this is not the flyer you sent to the printer."

"Of course it is. Why? Don't you like it?"

Ava put her head in her hands, moaning, "Oh, my God."

"What's wrong?"

"Jameson O'Rourke is on it!"

"I know. Isn't it great?"

"*Why* is Jameson on it?" she practically shrieked.

"Because he's the star of the show, silly."

"No, he's not, Steffy!"

"What do you mean he's not? I thought you'd asked him."

She hung her head. "Oh, dear God. Please tell me you didn't start distributing these yet."

"Umm. They're up all over town, Ava."

"Oh my God. Oh my God. Oh my God."

"What is wrong with you?"

The front door boomed open, and Ava looked up and through her office door to see the man in question storming in. He spotted her, strode through the empty front office, bee-lining straight for her. He stopped on the other side of her desk.

Her eyes swept over him. Dear Lord, he was so much more attractive in person than he was in those pictures, and that was saying something. Yes, she'd met him once before, but that was across a room, not leaning over her looking ready to grab her by the throat.

"They tell me you're the one responsible for this benefit bullshit thing. That true?"

She nodded, at a loss for words.

He held up a piece of paper clenched in his fist. "You want to explain how my name got on this flyer?"

The man was gorgeous and intimidating. She'd never been attracted to men with tattoos, and he was *covered*. Even with all that, there was no denying the man's appeal. He had it in spades, but he was also pissed — pissed at *her*. And that made him scary as hell.

Holy crap. She took a step back.

His eyes narrowed, waiting for her to speak.

"I'm so sorry. It was a misunderstanding," she began to explain.

"No, it *wasn't*," Stephanie insisted.

They both swung their gazes to her.

"Come again?" Jameson growled.

"You agreed to do it. I have your signed consent form."

"How is that possible, seeing as I never fucking signed one?"

Stephanie took a step back under the man's forceful gaze. "Your brother dropped it off. I have it right here."

She dug it out of a folder she was holding.

He grabbed it out of her hand and looked at the signature.

"I didn't sign this."

"That's your signature."

"No, it's not! Who did you say gave you this?"

"Your brother."

"I've got three. Which fucking one?"

"There's no need to snap at her," Ava intervened.

"I didn't catch his name. The one with the tattoos."

"That doesn't narrow it down any."

"He was built."

Jameson dipped his head, his eyes drilling into hers, clearly still not satisfied with her answer.

"Big guy, shorn hair, dark beard."

Jameson blew out a breath.

"Apparently we have a winner," Ava muttered under her breath.

His eyes snapped to hers. "Maxwell."

"So you're saying he signed your name to this form. Why would he do that?" Ava watched him run a frustrated hand through his hair.

"Probably thought it was funny. He's probably laughing his ass off right about now."

"You'll do it, won't you?" Stephanie asked.

He arched a brow. "Let you auction me off like a prize stud? Hell, no."

"Don't think of it like that. Think of it as going on a date for charity."

"If you think for one minute I'm going to get up on a stage and let women place bids on me, you've lost your goddamned mind."

"Please. You have to."

"I don't *have* to do anything, Cupcake," he growled, glaring at her.

"But... the flyers have already been printed. We've already sold out."

"*What?*" Both Jameson and Ava swung their astonished gazes toward Stephanie.

Her eyes darted between them. "We sold out in the first twenty-four hours. That's a record. And all because you're going to be the headliner."

"Not my problem," he ground out.

"Um, maybe we could work out a deal," Ava offered hesitantly, trying to find a way out of this without being sued.

His eyes swung to hers. "Deal? What kind of deal?"

"Maybe I could see that you get those parking spots you wanted."

That had him pulling back, his eyes narrowing as if

he just now recognized her.

"You're that bitch from the city council. It was you that turned everyone against me."

"She what?" Stephanie asked, frowning.

Jameson ignored her, his eyes still drilling into Ava's. "You hate that I have a shop on your precious Main Street. I know your kind. You're afraid I'll be bad for the town's image, that I'll attract the 'wrong' type of people, that I'll drive away your little *yuppie, farmer's market, coffee shop* crowd."

"Ava's not like that," Stephanie defended.

His eyes finally swung to Stephanie. "I tried to get designated motorcycle parking in front of my shop, and she shot it down."

Stephanie's eyes swung to her boss, questioningly. "Ava?"

"Steffy, stay out of this, please."

Jameson again pinned Ava with his eyes. "I sat through two and a half hours of that bullshit meeting, and you turned everyone in the room against me. So now I'm on the cover of a fucking magazine, and suddenly I'm the town's favorite son, and *you* need *me*. Seems the tables have turned, haven't they, sweetheart?"

Ava swallowed, ignoring the endearment he'd

used in anything but a flattering tone. She raised her chin. "We may have gotten off on the wrong foot, I admit, but—"

"Ya think?"

"As I was saying, I'm sure we can work something out. It is for charity, after all."

He glared at her, as if he knew she was trying to pull at his heartstrings. And then his eyes took in the office for the first time. "What is this place?"

"Hightower Staffing Services."

His chin lifted, considering. "Maybe we *can* work something out."

"Name it," Stephanie offered quickly.

Ava's eyes flashed to her, afraid she was about to get them in deeper.

"I've been having some trouble keeping a receptionist at the shop."

"Why am I not surprised?" Ava murmured under her breath.

"What the hell is that supposed to mean?"

She rolled her eyes ignoring his question. "So you want to hire us as your temp agency?"

"No. I don't want to hire you. I want you to send me over someone with no agency fee."

She arched a brow. "Really?"

"You want my time for free, don't you?"

"I'm already getting you parking spots!"

"That remains to be seen, doesn't it? No guarantee you'll be able to swing that vote back my way, is there?"

Her hands landed on her hips. "And there's no guarantee you'll do that auction, is there?"

He had the gall to grin at her.

"Here's the deal. You get me those parking spots *and* you keep someone qualified in the reception position from now until your gala, and I'll do your damn benefit auction. Deal?"

She cocked her head to the side. "What exactly is your definition of qualified? If you think for one minute that I'm going to rate my candidates based on their cup size, think again, Mister."

"Get real."

"I'm being real. If that's the kind of candidate you're looking for —"

"If that were the kind I was looking for, I've already got a stack of applications."

"So what's the problem?"

"Look, I get half a dozen women in the shop every week looking to 'land' the man they see on the cover of that magazine." He pointed to the copy of *Colorado Life* that was still lying on Ava's desk.

She glanced to where he pointed and flushed with embarrassment—humiliated that he saw she had it, like she was one of those women that fawned after him like some rock-star groupie.

"They see that and they see dollar signs."

"I think they see a whole lot more than dollar signs," Stephanie added with a grin.

"Not helpful, Steffy."

Jameson twisted to look at her. "Yeah, maybe so. But I'm not lookin' to date my employees, and that's all they're interested in." He turned back to face Ava. "What I need is someone with some maturity, who can add two plus two. Someone with some organizational skills, a pleasant phone manner, and yeah, if she's good lookin' that helps with the customers." He leaned forward, getting right in her face. "But despite what preconceived notions you may have about me, that's *not* on the top of my list."

"Okay, got it."

"Think you can deliver that kind of applicant?"

"I'm sure we have numerous candidates that would qualify."

"Fine. Have someone in the chair at 11:00 a.m. tomorrow morning."

"Did you want to interview them?"

"No. I'll trust your judgment. If I don't like them, I'll send them packing and expect you to send over a replacement within the hour."

"Within the hour? You can't be serious."

"As a heart attack, babe. We got a deal?"

Ava glanced at Stephanie, who nodded behind Jameson. Ava's eyes came back to the infuriating man, and then she stuck her hand out. "Fine. We have a deal."

He shook her hand, and then stalked out.

Ava collapsed into her chair.

Stephanie threw her hands in the air in victory. "Yes! We did it!"

Ava glared at her. "Don't be so quick to celebrate. We still have to deliver on our end of the bargain first, and I have a feeling Mr. O'Rourke is going to be a very difficult client to please."

"Hell, I'll go over there and do the job myself if I have to."

"Don't joke. It may come to that."

Stephanie rolled her eyes. "You worry too much."

"One of us has to. You better start pulling files. Find someone to send over tomorrow. And you'd better find at least two backups."

"Two?"

"Maybe three. How many do you think he can go through in one day?"

"You're being ridiculous. Why would we need to send three applicants? Have you seen the man? He's gorgeous. I wouldn't leave that job if he made me scrub the floors with a toothbrush."

"Oh, God. Do you think he'll want them to clean floors?"

"You're a hoot," Stephanie called as she walked out of the office.

Ava yelled down the hall after her, "We'll see who's laughing tomorrow!"

CHAPTER THREE

At 3:00 p.m. the next afternoon, the intercom on Ava's desk buzzed.

She pressed the button. "What is it?"

"Cover boy's on line two for you."

"What does he want?"

"Wouldn't say. Asked to speak with you."

Ava blew out a breath and picked up the phone, pressing line two. "Good afternoon, Mr. O'Rourke. What can I do for you?"

"Find me someone else."

"Is there a problem with the candidate we sent you?"

"Would I be calling if there wasn't?"

"Can you be more specific?"

"She's not working out."

"Are her computer skills adequate?"

"They're fine."

"Her phone manner?"

"It's fine."

"Was she on time this morning?"

"Yes. She was fifteen minutes early."

"Is she respectful? Organized? Able to add two plus two?" Okay now she was just being a smartass, but she couldn't help it.

"She's got a stick up her ass. I can't work with her. Find me someone else or the deal's off." The line cut off suddenly.

She pulled the receiver from her ear and stared at it, open-mouthed. How *rude*. She'd like to shove that stick up *his* ass!

She pushed the intercom button, and Stephanie's voice came on the line. "Yo."

"Who did you send over there?"

"Gail Reece. Why? No go?"

"He said she had a stick up her ass."

"Hmm. She does kind of have her nose in the air. I just thought she was the most qualified."

"Did she even want the position?"

"Not really. Took the assignment as more of a favor to me."

"Did you beg her?"

"Maybe a little."

Ava put her head in her hand. Gail was the most qualified office worker they had. The only reason she even needed a temp agency was because she only liked to take short-term assignments if and when she wanted to work. She had a husband who made enough so she didn't have to work if she didn't want to and only took jobs to make a little extra spending money and get out of the house.

"Find someone else."

"Gotcha."

"He's going to expect them over there today."

"Christ. I'm on it."

Ava hung up the receiver. She had a feeling this was only the beginning.

***

The next day she received another call from Jameson O'Rourke… and every day after that for five days straight. They were running out of candidates.

On Monday of the following week she was in the office working when the intercom buzzed.

She pressed the button. "Yes?"

"He sent another one packing," Stephanie said.

Ava closed her eyes. "You're kidding me?"

"Nope."

"What is with this guy?" Ava muttered, then asked, "Is this one in tears?"

"Yep."

"I'll be right there." Ava stood, shoved her chair

back, and marched out of her office. As she rounded the doorframe she could hear the sobbing coming from the reception area. Ava rushed into the front office to find the girl in tears.

"Victoria, what happened? Why are you crying?" She squatted down in front of the chair that Stephanie guided the girl to.

"He's h-h-horrible."

"Mr. O'Rourke?"

"Yes. Nothing I did was right. He yelled at me. I don't do well when people yell. I wasn't raised like that. I can't deal with it. I'm sorry, but I can't go back there."

"Of course not."

The phone rang, and Stephanie picked it up. "Hightower Staffing."

She put her hand over the phone and mouthed, "It's him."

Ava stood and marched toward her office. "Put him through!"

She yanked the receiver up and punched the button to connect the line. "Ava Hightower."

"You're joking right? That little church mouse you sent had no business working in a shop like mine."

"Now you listen here, Mr. O'Rourke. There is no

excuse for berating an employee."

"I'm Irish. I've got a temper. I blow off steam, and then it's over. If you can't find me someone with more backbone by the time the shop opens tomorrow, the deal is off. I don't have time to train girl after girl on our computer system just to have them quit on me."

"Quit on you? You've sent them all packing!"

"Same difference. You're wasting my time. Find me someone capable by tomorrow morning or you can forget about me strutting down any fucking runway. I don't care how deserving the damn charity is!"

With that he hung up.

She stared at the phone in her hand again in outrage, and then slammed it down. "Blast that man!"

Stephanie came to lean on the doorframe with her arms folded. "I seriously didn't think it would be this difficult."

"*He's* the one being difficult. Why he's nothing but an overgrown child demanding it be his way or the highway."

"What are we going to do? I've used up everyone we've got available."

Ava shrugged. "Guess you're going to have to go work for him like you offered to do when we got into this mess."

"Umm. That's a problem."

Ava's shoulders slumped. "What do you mean? You promised if worse came to worst you'd do it yourself."

"I got called for jury duty tomorrow, remember?"

Ava dropped her head. "Crap. I forgot."

"I can try to get out of it, but I could be there most of the day before that happens."

"No. Of course you have to go."

"What are we going to do about Jameson O'Rourke?"

Ava rolled her eyes. "I guess that just leaves me."

"You're serious? You're really going to go work the front counter at a tattoo shop?"

"Why not? It's honest work. I'm certainly capable."

"You have a Master's degree in Human Resources."

"I need to make the client happy. I can certainly stick it out for..." She paused to look at the calendar. Oh, my God. She'd be there for six weeks.

"Maybe in a few days we can get someone else."

"Nope. He said whomever I send tomorrow had to stick it out till the end or the deal was off. He was sick of training every new girl we sent."

"So, you're saying you'd have to be that girl for the

next six weeks?"

"You see any other option? Please tell me."

"Ava, I'm so sorry. I know you can't stand the man."

"I'll just have to buck up. How bad can it be?"

If only she'd known just how prophetic those words would be.

CHAPTER FOUR

The next day, Ava worked at the agency from 7:00 until 10:30. Then she closed up the office and headed down the street the short two-block walk to Brothers Ink on Main Street.

The closed sign was hanging in the window, but she could see some movement in the back of the shop. She took a deep breath and knocked on the glass. A few moments later, she could make out the outline of a big man with a beard as he came to the door and spoke through the glass in a muffled voice.

"We're closed. Come back in a half hour, honey."

"I'm not a customer. I'm your new receptionist," Ava replied in a voice hopefully loud enough for him to hear.

He paused, a frown forming on his face as his eyes skated down her body and back up. Then he reached up to flip the bolt.

The door swung open. "Come on in."

She stepped in, her eyes immediately scanning the décor. The shop was a two-story brick building that dated from the turn of the century. It apparently had been gutted down to the gleaming wood floors and exposed brick walls and totally remodeled, but still leaving that old character that fit so well in the Colorado town. A huge chrome sculpture of a buffalo sat in the entrance and there was a large seating area.

Ava's eyes couldn't help but travel around the room. It was a classy set up. Since there were no customers at the moment, she assumed the four bikes outside must belong to the O'Rourke brothers.

She'd heard that Jameson viewed what he did as an art form. That certainly was reflected not only in the décor of the shop that felt more like an art gallery than any tattoo shop she'd ever imagined, but also by the fact that the place was lined with framed art. All of it, she'd heard, was Jameson's.

The place was impressive, sleek, and modern. A reception counter stood across the entrance, tattoo stations lined behind it. No one stood at the counter.

She could see, at the back of the shop, an open staircase that led to the second floor.

The man held out his hand. "I'm Maxwell... or Max for short."

She shook his hand. "Hello, Max. I'm Ava. Ava Hightower."

He nodded as he continued to hold her hand. "Ava. Pretty name. And you're our new girl?"

"It would seem so."

They both turned at the sound of the back door opening. Ava looked over Max's shoulder and down the back hall to see another man walking in. He was almost as big as this one.

Max twisted before turning back to her. "That's my brother, Liam."

Liam came to stand next to Max, his arms folded. "This the latest one?"

Ava studied the two. Both were big, muscular, and covered in ink. They also both had brown eyes and beards, although Liam's hair was a golden brown that fell to his collar and was tucked behind an ear.

"Liam, this is Ava."

The man extended his hand. "Ava."

She shook it. "Hello, Liam."

He released her hand, his eyes sweeping over her before returning to his brother. "Jamie in yet?"

"He's upstairs."

"You tell him she's here?"

Max's eyes returned to her, and he smiled as he answered his brother. "Not yet."

Liam grinned as if there was some inside joke she

wasn't in on. "Let me do the honors."

Ava watched as he walked to the open staircase near the back and hollered up. "Jamie, get your ass down here."

Max twisted to look over his shoulder. "Nice, Liam. Real subtle, and watch the swearing. There's a lady present."

Liam just grinned back as he strolled over to one of the tattoo stations and sat in the chair. He leaned back, folding his hands behind his head. "This should be good."

Ava frowned at him. "What do you mean?"

"Never mind him." Max held his arm out toward the reception area. "Why don't you put your things down? Can I get you a cup of coffee?"

"Why yes, I'd love a cup."

The sound of boots tromping down the stairs echoed through the place, and they both turned to watch Jameson O'Rourke approach. He stopped short when he saw her.

"What are you doing here?"

"She's our new receptionist," Max added helpfully.

"Like hell she is," he snapped at Max before turning back to her. "You want to explain."

She raised her chin as she shrugged out of her

raincoat and tossed it over the chair. "He's right."

His eyes swept over her. "Uh, no. No way in hell, sweetheart."

"Excuse me. Why not?"

He lifted a hand, gesturing to her outfit. "You really gotta ask?"

She glanced down at her outfit. It was the one she'd worn to her own office this morning, a tasteful cream business skirt and a silk blouse in a pretty cream and gold print. She'd topped it off with a gold chain belt and a pair of suede pumps. It went well with her blonde hair that was pulled up in a French twist. Her hands landed on her hips. "What's wrong with what I'm wearing?"

"Not a thing from what I can see," Max put in with a grin and a wink. "I think she looks beautiful."

Jameson gave him a look that told him to shut up. "Don't you have work to do?"

"Sure. But this is too much fun."

"Second that," Liam added with a chuckle from behind them.

Jameson twisted to glare at him before turning back to her. "Seriously, what are you doing here? Did you come to concede the fact that you couldn't keep up your end of the bargain?"

She folded her arms. *What a jerk!* "I'm not here to do any such thing. I intend to uphold my end of our bargain. You need someone to work your reception. And since none of the candidates I've already sent you have been acceptable to you, here I am."

Jameson folded his arms. "Don't you have your own business to run? I'd think between that and your position on the city council, you'd have your hands full."

"I'll manage. Right now, you are my number one priority, Mr. O'Rourke."

"Jameson."

"Fine. Jameson."

He moved toward her until he was in her space — so close she had to refrain from taking a step back. She lifted her chin as he dipped his head until he was practically nose-to-nose with her. Two sets of blue eyes faced off. With a quiet, but deceptively commanding voice, he stated, "Well, sweetheart, as much as I love hearing I'm a woman's number one priority, I think you've bitten off more than you can chew."

She smirked. "I hardly think so."

"You do realize this is a tattoo shop, right?"

"Of course I do."

"And you understand our clientele are hardly the

silk blouse crowd?" He lifted his chin toward her outfit.

She rolled her eyes.

"Rule number one, don't roll your eyes at me, sweetheart."

She ground her teeth and snapped, "*Don't* call me sweetheart. *My* rule."

"You don't get any rules. This is my shop."

"Come on, Jamie. The girl wants to wear a skirt and heels, I'm all for it," Liam put in as he stretched back in his chair, clearly attempting to diffuse the rapidly escalating situation.

Jameson's eyes drilled into her. "You're serious about taking this position? Because I told you on the phone, this is the last time I'm training someone. So, are you really willing to stick this out to the end, *Ms. Hightower?*"

"I'm perfectly serious."

"And what about your own business?"

"I'll work there in the morning until you open up at 11:00, then I'll come here."

"We're open 'till 9:00. And sometimes we're here long after that finishing up with customers and cleaning the shop. How long are you going to be able to keep those hours up?"

"I'll manage."

He studied her almost contemplatively. "Rule number two. I don't want to hear any bitching or complaining. I've got no patience for high-maintenance prima donnas. Understood?"

She practically had to grit her teeth to keep from snapping at him. "Understood."

Jameson stared her down, and then finally grabbed a chair and rolled it over next to her reception desk. He motioned her toward the other chair. "Then let's go over the computer system. And I'm not going to repeat everything, so listen up the first time."

CHAPTER FIVE

Ava threw her pen on the counter. It had been three days since she'd started working at Brothers Ink and each day was more frustrating than the one before.

Jameson O'Rourke had the most backwards, archaic computer system she'd ever seen. Everything had to be entered separately; nothing connected. Appointment information didn't cross with billing information. The whole system was an antiquated hot mess. It made her want to chuck the monitor off her desk.

No wonder the girls she'd sent over had such a hard time. This system was a nightmare. Why in God's name hadn't he ever upgraded the software? Was the man computer illiterate? She'd had clients before with systems they dreaded replacing just for the simple fact that they were familiar with their current system and hated change or having to retrain. But this was ridiculous.

It was a time consuming, inefficient nightmare. She could think of three programs off the top of her head that would be much more effective and would work beautifully for his needs.

Then there were the photo files. What a mess *they* were. Tattoo artists kept photos of all their work, she'd learned, and those photos were uploaded to the computer system. Sure, she could understand the practice in theory. But in reality, nothing was easy to find, none of them were named in a systematic way in order to make them easily searchable. Nope, the brothers just named them with whatever came to mind, such as, Cool Red Dragon or Butterfly on Chick's Hip. *Seriously?*

And they were *surprised* when they couldn't remember what they'd called it? Shocking! *Well, newsflash, boys, things were about to change.*

Ava stood from her chair and marched back toward the stairs. She felt the eyes of Max and Liam follow her as she passed by their stations. She'd yet to meet the youngest of the four brothers, but heard he was due back from a trip and would be in later today.

She marched up the stairs, her heels clicking on the wood. She knew Jameson's office was at the top, but she'd never actually been up there yet. Max and Liam each had a client in their chairs and there wasn't another appointment until after lunch, so she felt safe running up to speak with Jameson for a moment.

She climbed to the top of the open staircase and found the entire floor was an open-plan room, and all of it was Jameson's office. Framed sketches of some of his art lined the walls. A large modern glass desk sat at the front of the building.

Jameson was sitting at the desk, sketching on a pad, a large picture window behind him.

"May I speak with you for a moment, Jameson?"

His head lifted, his eyes running over her. "Aren't you supposed to be manning the front?"

"I'll hear the bell above the door."

"And the phones?"

"They haven't rung all morning. This will just take a moment."

"All right. Shoot."

Don't tempt me. "It's about the computer system."

He dropped the pencil he'd been sketching with. "Don't tell me you messed it up again."

Her hands landed on her hips. "No, I didn't 'mess it up' again."

"Then what?"

"The system is ancient. I can suggest several new programs that would be much more efficient and suit your needs better than the one you're currently using."

"There's nothing wrong with the system."

"There's plenty wrong with that system."

"It's served our needs since we opened this shop. It's fine."

"And how long ago was that?"

"What, when we opened?"

"Yes."

He shrugged. "I was nineteen."

"Correct me if I'm wrong, but wasn't that decades ago?"

His chin came up. "You fishing to find out how old I am, Slick?"

"I know how old you are. Thirty-eight."

He leaned back in his chair. "Really? Which magazine article did you get that from?"

"Does it matter? It's correct, isn't it?"

"It's correct."

"Your age is irrelevant. It's the age of your computer software that is shocking."

"Shocking?" His brows rose.

"Surely I can't be the first person to point this out to you."

He rose from his seat so suddenly she took a step back. "My software is none of your damn concern. I didn't hire you for a business consultation."

"You didn't hire me at all, Superstar," she snapped

back.

"You done with the smartass comments? Deal was you work here until your fancy Gala, end of story. Not complain about every little thing in this place. I don't want or need your advice on how I run my business, got it? Now get back to work."

She pivoted on her heel and stalked toward the staircase. "You're insufferable."

***

Max's eyes followed as Ava angrily stalked back to the front counter. He'd heard their muffled voices carrying down the stairs as she and Jameson had yet another confrontation. Returning his attention to his work, he put the final touches on the tattoo he was doing until he was completely satisfied with the design.

"That should do it." Switching off his machine, he picked up a hand mirror and held it up, positioning the image in the reflection. "Tell me what you think?"

The twenty-three-year-old girl in his chair gazed at the intricate floral and dove motif they'd worked together to design. "Oh, wow. It's gorgeous."

Max smiled at her. "Glad you like it. I think it represents your mother's memory well, don't you?"

At that, she got a bit teary-eyed. "Yes. Thank you."

"My pleasure, honey." He took the mirror from her

hand and set it down, then grabbed a tissue and handed it to her. She took it with a shy smile and dabbed her eyes while he reached for some ointment. He smeared it over the ink, gently bandaged it, and explained tattoo aftercare to her.

It had been her first tattoo, and she'd done beautifully. Of course, he'd had to talk her through her initial fears and nervousness in the beginning, but she'd taken the needle like a champ. Pulling off his black surgical gloves, he extended his hand, helping her from the chair, and then led her to the front to pay.

After she'd paid and left, he glanced over at the frown on Ava's face as she tucked the money she'd collected from his customer away in the cash drawer.

"What's wrong?" he asked.

"It's nothing. It's just that some things around here don't make any sense to me."

"What things?"

"Cash only. How can any business survive being cash only in this day and age?" she asked, turning to him.

He shrugged. "Jamie doesn't want to pay the fee the banks charge to take the cards. Says it's highway robbery. They didn't do shit, so why should they get any percentage?"

She gave him a look.

"Hey, just repeating what the man said."

"Unbelievable. How does one run a business like this?"

"The shop has a pretty good reputation. If people want a tattoo from us, they come up with the cash." He tilted his head to the side. "You hungry?"

She frowned. "What?"

"Let's take a walk. I'll buy you an ice cream."

"But it's not my dinner break."

He waggled his brows. "Let's be real rebels and rule breakers."

"But… the phones."

"Liam can cover 'em."

"Jameson will kill me."

"I guarantee you, he won't."

"But…"

"Come on, pretty girl. You could use a break."

She huffed out a breath. "I suppose you're right."

They walked a block down the quaint main street to an ice cream place. A large six-foot-tall ice cream cone made from what probably was fiberglass stood by the door, beckoning passersby to stop. After ordering, they sat at a small wrought iron table out front.

"You have to understand something about Jamie,

and the reason he is the way he is." Max looked at her.

"Rude and insufferable?" She smirked, scooping up a spoon of Rocky Road from her paper cup.

He grinned, taking a lick from his waffle cone. "I won't argue that one, but Jamie's had to fight for everything. Our parents died in a car accident when he was just eighteen."

She slowly pulled the spoon from her mouth, shocked by what Maxwell had just revealed. "I'm so sorry. I had no idea."

He nodded. "I was fifteen, Liam was ten, and Rory was seven. And suddenly Jameson was responsible for all of us."

"Oh my God." Her brow pulled together with concern.

"Yeah."

"Wasn't there anyone to take you in? An aunt or uncle or grandparents?"

"Grandparents were dead. Had one aunt in Boston, but she was sick with MS, and it would have been too much for her. So Jameson stepped up. Had to fight like hell to prove to social services that we were better off with him in our own home than broken up among different foster homes. He swore to us that would never happen, and he made sure it didn't."

"I see."

"Do you? Jameson was supposed to go off to school that fall. He gave it all up to keep the family together. Everything he's ever done has been for us."

Ava thought about what Max was telling her, trying to make it fit with the man she thought she knew. "How did he end up tattooing?"

"He'd played around with it as a teenager, much to our mother's annoyance. After the accident, he got this guy he'd met to show him everything about laying ink. Figured it was a marketable skill — one he could make more money from than any minimum wage job he'd be qualified for. We lived off what little insurance money there was while Jamie learned the skill. Every day he'd make sure we did our homework, he'd make us dinner, and then he'd go to Pete's shop every night and tattoo while I put Liam and Rory to bed.

"The next morning, no matter how late he'd gotten home, Jamie would get us up for school, feed us breakfast, and make sure we caught the bus. Then he'd go work a shitty day job at the Ryerson's Feed & Seed, shoveling feed until 5:00.

"My point is, he's scrimped and saved and busted his ass to provide for his brothers. We owe him everything. So when a bank wants to take three percent, or four percent, or whatever the going rate is now to run a debit card, I get why he doesn't think they deserve any of his hard earned money."

"But...things are better now. Aren't they? I mean he's on the cover of all those magazines and that TV show..."

"Yeah. Things are better now. Things are easy, for the first time in years, but old habits die hard. He's had to scrape by and hold the reins so tight, it's not easy for him to let go."

Max watched as she looked off into the distance, gazing at the people walking by and the cars driving past, and he could tell she was absorbing all the information he'd just given her.

"I judged your brother unfairly, knowing basically nothing about him."

"So maybe you'll take that all into consideration the next time he pisses you off and acts like a controlling jerk. It's not that he's trying to be an ass, that's just him trying to hold onto his family."

She nodded. "Thank you for telling me."

"You let on I told you any of that shit, Jamie will kill me."

She grinned. "I understand. I won't say a word."

He reached out and tugged on a lock of her hair.

"Don't stop bein' you. Keep givin' him shit. Keep pushin' your ideas. It's good for him." He paused, considering. "I think *you're* good for him."

"Me?"

He nodded. "Yep. You."

"He and I are like oil and water."

"They do say opposites attract, and I definitely think somebody needs to shake Jameson up."

"And I'm the girl to do it?"

He shrugged. "Maybe. One thing Jameson has no patience for is stupidity. Intelligence, for him, is the ultimate sexy trait, and smartass sarcasm reveals intelligence. Don't think for a minute he doesn't notice and appreciate yours."

She rolled her eyes. "You're delusional. The only thing that man thinks of me is that I'm a pain in his ass. This is a business arrangement, that's all. He gets his parking spots and someone in his receptionist chair, and I get someone to do my Gala. That's all there is to this."

"If you say so." He stood. "Better get back to the shop."

***

"Where the hell have you two been?" Jameson snapped the moment they were through the front door.

"I took her for ice cream," Max replied calmly, loving that this was getting Jameson riled up.

Jameson's brow arched. "You took her for ice cream?"

Max grinned. "Yup."

Jameson glared back at him and lifted his chin. "Break room. Now." Then his gaze swung to Ava. "You. Back to work."

She saluted him. "Yes, Sir."

"And don't be a smartass."

Max watched Jameson retreat and winked at Ava before following the man.

Jameson slammed the door open and moved to lean against the counter, his arms folded. Max strolled to the refrigerator and took out an energy drink.

"Didn't you just have a bunch of sugar?" Jameson's eyes dropped to the can.

Max popped the top with a wild look on his face. "I like to live dangerously."

"What the fuck was that all about?"

"What the fuck was *what* all about?"

"*You*. Takin' her for ice cream."

He shrugged. "She needed a break."

"She needs a break, she can come in here. She's a big girl. She doesn't need you holding her hand."

"You want to tell me why you're being such a dick to her?"

"I'm not being a dick." Jameson looked away, his eyes making a liar of him.

"The hell you're not. You've been riding her ass since she walked in the door. So what the fuck is going on?"

Jameson took a deep breath and blew it out, shaking his head. "I have no intention of walking a damn catwalk in any damn bachelor auction. That's what."

"So why'd you agree to it?"

"She has to fulfill her end of the bargain first. That's not going to happen."

Max's chin came up. He hadn't expected his brother to go into this bet dishonestly. "You're going to make sure she doesn't."

"Exactly."

"So, what? You're trying to run her ass off?"

"Yup."

"Jameson, that's playin' fucking dirty."

"Maybe."

"Ain't no maybe about it."

"What do you care?"

"I like her."

"No, you just want to see me up on that fucking stage."

Max grinned. "That, too."

"Well, it's not happening. So don't hold your breath. Last thing I'm gonna do is lose this game." With that he stalked out, slamming into Liam's shoulder as he walked in.

Liam turned his head, his eyes following Jameson, and then he looked at Max. "What the fuck is his problem?"

"Ava."

"Ava? What's not to like about Ava?"

"Exactly." Max grinned. "He is so fucking screwed."

CHAPTER SIX

That evening, Ava was busy reorganizing the photo files, her eyes intent on her computer screen when the front door opened and a man strode in. He didn't stop at the reception counter, but walked past her toward the tattoo stations.

She twisted in her chair, her eyes following him. He paused next to Liam's station. Straightening from his customer, Liam glanced up at the man, and then grinned. "How'd it go?"

The man slid his hands in the hip pockets of his low hanging jeans, and Ava's eyes moved up over the tattoos that ran up both of his arms.

"Fantastic. Filled every show." He turned his head, his eyes connecting with hers as he asked Liam, "Who's the new chick?"

Ava watched Liam's eyes drop to her, and he grinned. He wiped a cloth over the ink he was laying and bent back over his customer's bicep, applying the needle to skin. The buzzing filled the space again, but she could still hear his reply. "That's Ava, our new receptionist. She's a sweetheart, so don't be an ass."

The man grinned, his brow pulling up as he put a palm to his chest. "Me, an ass? I'm wounded, Brother."

Liam's eyes flicked over to her, and he shouted, "Hey, Ava. Come meet my little brother."

At that, she had no choice but to get up from her chair and walk over. As she approached, the man turned toward her. Her eyes fell to his extended hand. Silver bracelets encircled his wrist, rings on his fingers. Her gaze skated up over him until they connected with his eyes, *dark piercing eyes* with slashing brows. He had long dark hair that hung past his shoulders and a beard that ran along his jawbone and framed his mouth. The whole look reminded Ava of a rock star. *Or perhaps a pirate,* she mused. She extended her hand, and he took it in his, but instead of shaking it, he brought it to his lips.

"Ava, pretty name for a pretty lady. I'm Rory."

"Don't you have enough women falling at your feet, Bro? Don't hit on our receptionist. She's actually managed to last the week without Jameson running her off."

Rory's eyes moved to Liam and then back to her, and his brows rose. "Really? My pain-in-the-ass older brother hasn't had you running for the hills, yet?

Amazing. Although, I can't imagine why he'd give such a lovely lady a hard time."

"Rory, what'd I just say?" Liam reminded him.

Rory looked at her, his white teeth flashing into a gorgeous smile. "My brother likes to suck all the fun out of life."

She smiled back at him as he finally released her hand. "It's nice to finally meet you, Rory. Have you been on vacation?"

"I was out of town, but I wouldn't call it a vacation. Had a week-long gig in Salt Lake."

"Gig?"

"Rory plays in a band," Liam filled in for her. "And I *would* call that a vacation."

"Ah." She nodded, her eyes sweeping over him. "The rock star look makes sense, then."

Rory grinned. "A rock star, huh? You hear that, Bro?"

Liam cut in. "Don't tell him that, Ava. His head's too big already."

She chuckled. "Oh, is it?"

"Yep. He's got groupies and everything. Now if only he could actually *make a living at it*," Liam finished in a teasing voice.

"I do okay."

"Right. You're lucky if your cut covers your bar tab."

"Well, one day, sooner than you think, it's gonna set us all up."

"Yeah, well, I'm not holding my breath on that."

"See the love and support I get, Ava?"

She giggled at his teasing. "And what instrument do you play?"

"Guitar."

"Do you sing as well?"

"We all sing. But I'm not usually the lead." He stepped closer. "We've got a local show coming up soon. You'll have to come see us."

"I'd like that."

Liam looked up from his customer again, his eyes meeting Rory's. "Don't you have an 8:00 you need to be getting set up for?"

Rory grinned and turned, heading back to the supply room.

Liam glanced up at Ava. "Be warned. Rory's a bit of a flirt, sweetheart."

She grinned down at him. "Oh, and you're not?"

"See, I knew you had beauty *and* brains." He winked, and she shook her head, laughing. The bell over the door tinkled, and she turned to look as three leather-clad men entered. Ava recognized them right away as bikers, and she straightened, stiffening as her eyes swept over them. They were big and bearded and scary as crap.

Liam must have sensed her immediate unease, for she heard him murmur something to his customer about giving him a minute, and then he was clicking off his machine and rising from his stool. He brushed up against her back, dipping his head close to whisper, "I got this, sweetness. Relax."

He moved past her to greet the men.

She quickly moved behind the high reception counter and sat at her computer, giving it her full attention and trying to ignore the way they checked her out. But she kept them in the corner of her eye, watching as Liam stood talking with them.

"Ryder."

"Liam."

"Rory finishing your sleeve tonight?"

"That's the plan." The man's eyes flicked over Liam's shoulder, searching. "He here?"

Liam nodded, twisting to look behind him. "He's in the back getting some needle cartridges and inks. How are things going with you?"

"Same old, same old." The man's eyes skated to

Ava, and she couldn't help but glance over. "New girl?"

"New receptionist."

The man lifted his chin. "You boys sure go through 'em around here. What happened to the last one? The dark haired one we all liked."

"Crystal? Dude, she was about ten receptionists ago."

"Huh." The man studied Ava.

"She went back to Cali," Liam continued explaining, drawing his attention back off her. "Why don't you go ahead and get in the chair?"

Rory ambled out of the supply room. "Hey, man. Come on back."

Ava watched as the biker walked off, then her gaze flicked over to see the two men he'd come in with still standing there. One took a seat. The other moved to lean on the counter, grinning down at her.

"Hey, girlie."

Her eyes darted from him to Liam.

Liam's gaze moved between them. "You okay, Ava?"

"I'm fine."

"You need me, call."

She nodded.

The man's eyes flicked up to Liam. "She ain't gonna need you."

"I'm fine, Liam," Ava insisted.

Liam returned to his customer.

The biker stared down at her again. "So, you're new, huh?"

"I've been here a while."

"I ain't seen you before."

"No, I'm sure I'd remember you as well."

He grinned. "Would you, now?"

She gave him a smile that didn't reach her eyes. "Yes, you smell like motor oil."

His grin faded. "You're a sassy little thing, aren't you?"

She shrugged.

"That's okay. I like a woman with sass."

"Were you getting tattooed as well?"

"Not tonight. But seein' you here makes me think I might be back real soon."

Oh joy. She could hardly wait. Ava stared up at him, giving him a look that left no mistake she wished he'd move away from her counter and go sit down. Unfortunately, he didn't seem to be taking the hint. As they studied each other, she took in every detail.

He was bald, with a goatee and a scar along his

mouth. There was a tiny teardrop tattoo next to his eye. Her gaze moved down to notice the ink that covered his neck. It looked like some type of dagger with the word luck across it and what looked like blood dripping down onto a big tarantula. The whole thing scared the hell out of her.

Her eyes flicked back up to his. They were empty, soulless eyes. She swallowed and searched her brain for some remark that would get him to lose interest and go away, but just then Max walked up to stand behind her. She tilted her head back to meet his eyes, and she knew he could see the uneasiness and—yes, she'd admit it— *fear* in hers, and she wondered if the biker had seen it, too.

Max put his hand on her shoulder and squeezed. "Let's go over those photo files again."

She knew he didn't need to go over anything with her. He was just doing this to have a reason to be standing up here with her. She nodded mutely and turned toward her computer screen. With shaking hands, she pulled up a file folder and clicked it open, bringing up a screen full of photo files. She felt Max lean over her, one hand on the counter, the other on the back of her chair. His big presence had never felt more comforting.

"I-I wasn't sure how you wanted to organize this group," she whispered up at him and saw him twist his head to speak to the biker.

"You might as well take a seat. Your friend's gonna be a while."

The biker stared at him a moment, then pushed off the counter in frustration and moved away. But he didn't sit down; instead he walked over to Rory's station to watch his MC brother get his ink.

Ava glanced up, her eyes meeting Max's, and she mouthed the words, "Thank you."

He winked at her, and then nodded at her computer monitor.

***

As closing time drew near and the bikers seemed to be leaving Ava alone, Max squeezed her shoulder. "You gonna be okay? I need to go clean up my station and restock."

She stared up at him and smiled, grateful to him for looking out for her the way he had. "I'll be fine. Thank you."

He patted her shoulder and walked away.

Ava began straightening her work area. A few minutes later, Rory walked the biker he'd been working on up to the front counter to pay. He glanced over at Ava. "He's $250, sweetheart."

She nodded and began printing out a bill.

"I don't need a receipt," the man informed her, slapping the bills down on the counter.

"All right." She gathered up the money, noticing the other scary biker was now standing next to Rory's customer, staring intently at her. It made her hands shake as she quickly counted up the bills. It didn't help that Jameson walked up as she was doing it. Five sets of eyes watched her shaking hands.

Leaning on the end of the counter, Rory exchanged a few words with his customer, breaking the tension. "You decide on the design for your shoulder, give me a call, man."

"Will do." The customer's eyes moved to Jameson. "Got something I want to add to that back design you did for me."

Jameson nodded. "I'm booked up the next few weeks. Were you in a hurry to get it done?"

"Nah. I've got to go out of town for a while. I'll call and set something up when I get back."

"Sounds good."

The biker's eyes skated to Ava. "We square?"

"Yes, sir. Thank you," she murmured quickly as she put the money away in the cash drawer.

Rory extended his hand to the man, and they shook. The bikers ambled out the front door. When they were gone, he walked over and locked the door, flipping the OPEN sign to CLOSED.

Jameson moved to stand in front of the counter, his palms flat on the Formica, his arms splayed. Ava felt uncomfortable as he studied her closely.

"You got a problem with our clientele, Princess?"

She knew he had noticed her shaking hands. She also knew he was just trying to get to her, and her chin came up. "Not at all. And don't call me that."

Jameson stared her down. "You want to quit, you want out of this deal, say the word."

"You'd like that, wouldn't you?"

"You bet I would."

"It's not happening."

"We'll see about that, sweetheart."

"What's that supposed to mean?"

"It means six weeks is a long time, babe."

She turned away and noticed Rory's eyes dart between her and Jameson, but he thankfully didn't say anything. The last thing she wanted was to give Jameson something else to ride her about. If he thought his brothers were catering to her in any way, he'd throw that in her face, too. She already felt like he watched her like a hawk, waiting for any excuse to pounce with another reason why she wasn't up to snuff.

Finally, Jameson turned to Rory. "Get your station cleaned up, I want to get out of here."

Rory nodded as Jameson shoved from the counter and strode to the back of the shop, taking the stairs to his office. Ava's eyes followed him.

"Hey."

Her eyes swung back to Rory.

"Don't let him get to you. He's just trying to push your buttons."

She nodded and felt a sting to her eyes. Blinking, she turned back to straighten her work area, but Rory must have noticed the sheen of tears she fought, because a moment later she felt his palm settle over her shoulder giving it a squeeze before he too, moved off.

When he was gone, she tapped the bottom edge of a stack of supplier invoices on the counter, straightening them, and then set them in a file folder. Her hands moved busily around her area as she silently fumed. She realized she was overreacting and the truth of it was, Jameson had hit a little too close with his question. She *was* uncomfortable with some of their clientele. That man earlier had scared her, more than she wanted to let on. But she'd be damned if she'd give Jameson the satisfaction of knowing it.

Shoving her chair in, she walked to the break room to empty out her coffee mug. When she'd washed it out, she wiped down the counter.

Max poked his head in. "Ava, you parked in back? I'm headed out. I'll walk you to your car."

She twisted, glancing over her shoulder and giving him a smile. "I'm out on the street. But thanks and have a good night."

"Okay, doll. Liam's up talking with Jamie, but make sure Rory walks you out."

"I'm sure I'll be fine."

"Company policy. Someone walks you out. Got it?"

"Got it."

"See you tomorrow then."

"Bye, Max."

He slapped the wall and walked out.

She finished up and walked back up front. Rory was just finishing straightening his station. "You ready to go, doll?"

"Yes, just let me grab my purse."

He walked her out the front, pausing to lock the door. Then he turned to her. "Where are you parked?"

She pointed down the block and they started

walking.

"So what's the deal with you and my brother?" Rory asked.

She turned to look at him. "Which brother?"

He chuckled. "You know which brother. Jamie."

She blew out a breath. "He doesn't much care for me, does he?"

"I wouldn't say that." He grinned.

It was her turn to laugh. "Right."

"Let's just say there's some strong emotions flying around the shop. What I want to know is why."

She shrugged. "I'm on the city council. I voted against him getting those parking spots. Well, more than voted. I sort of rallied the council to shoot it down."

Rory let out a huff of laughter.

Ava looked at him curiously. "That's funny?"

"My brother getting shot down by a woman? Yeah, it's a riot. Damn, I wished I'd have been there to see that."

"I take it that doesn't happen very often."

"No, ma'am. You may be a first."

"Lucky me."

At that he burst out laughing again.

She stopped in front of her car, sliding the key in

the lock. "This is me."

He waited while she opened the door and climbed in. With his hand on the frame, he leaned in. "Don't let him get you down, Ava. His bark is worse than his bite."

"I'll keep that in mind."

"Drive safe."

"I will. Thanks."

He stepped back, shutting her door, and she fired up the engine. She watched him turn and head back toward the shop as she pulled out onto the street, rolling down to the light at the corner. She stopped, waiting for the light to change when something in her peripheral vision caught her attention. Turning, she saw the flare of a cigarette as someone who stood in the shadows, leaning against the building on the corner, took a draw off it. The glow illuminated the man's face for a brief second. But that was all it took for recognition to hit her.

It was the scary biker from earlier. His eyes stared right at her. She quickly turned away, praying the light would change. A second later, she glanced back and he was gone. That had her head turning to the right, her eyes darting all around the street, trying to find him. A sudden knock on her driver's window scared the crap out of her and had her jerking her head back to the left. She looked up and he was standing right there. She felt her stomach drop as he motioned for her to roll the window down. *Not on your life, buddy.*

She glanced back at the light, preparing to run it, regardless, when finally it changed, and she stomped on the gas. She looked in her rearview mirror. The man was still standing in the street watching her drive away, and then he was jogging across the street. She imagined he was headed to wherever his bike was parked. She drove as fast as she could straight home, her eyes on her rearview mirror the entire way, but no one followed her.

With her cell phone clutched in her hand, she hurried from her car to her front door. Quickly fumbling with the key, she made it inside and threw the bolt. Peering through the curtain, she watched the street, but no traffic went past. Sighing with relief, she tossed her handbag on the couch, kicked off her shoes, and headed into the kitchen to get a drink.

She took a glass down and held it under the icemaker as her thumb moved over her cell phone screen. A moment later, she put it to her ear, listening to the dial tone as she poured some juice into her glass.

Stephanie's voice came on the line. "Hey, sweetie.

What's up?"

Ava tucked the phone between her ear and shoulder as she dug into her cookie jar. "Nothing. Just checking in. How are things at the office?"

Stephanie yawned. "Same old, same old. How goes it with the boss from hell?"

"He's still his irritable self. I swear nothing pleases that man."

"Come on, he can't be that bad?"

"Oh, no? Come by after work tomorrow. You can see for yourself."

"I thought you'd never ask. I'm dying to come see."

Ava munched on a cookie and stared at the ceiling. "We had a big blowout today."

"Over what?"

"I suggested he upgrade his computer system."

"I'm guessing he didn't take too well to that idea."

"Nope. Bit my head off. I swear, that man is the most frustrating person to work for. It's his way or the highway."

"Well, unfortunately, you can't let it be the highway in this case, so you're just gonna have to suck it up."

"I'm well aware. But it's a lot harder than I thought it would be."

"I wish there was something I could do to help."

"Come by tomorrow. Maybe he'll see you and let you take my spot."

"Hmm. Now I'm not sure I want to work there. You make it sound so terrible."

"Steffy!"

"Well, you *do!*"

Ava smiled. She knew what would tempt Steffy into coming down. She wouldn't be able to keep her away, in fact. "Did I tell you I finally got to meet the youngest of the O'Rourke brothers today?"

"No, you didn't. Is he an asshole like his big brother?"

"He's in a rock band." Ava could literally feel Steffy's sudden interest perk up.

"What?"

"Yeah. He's in the band, Convicted Chrome. And oh my God, Steffy, he's gorgeous."

"Oh my God! No way! What does he look like? Does he play guitar? Does he sing?"

Ava grinned. She knew she had her then, hook, line, and sinker. "He's Rock God gorgeous. And yes, he sings *and* plays guitar.

"Okay, that's it. You sold me. I'll be over after work tomorrow. And you better not be exaggerating, Sister!"

Ava grinned. "See you tomorrow."

As she disconnected the call, her doorbell rang. Glancing down the hall, she stared at the front door and immediately thought of the biker. Had he followed her home, and she just didn't see him? She hesitated, not wanting to answer. But she couldn't stop herself from moving toward the door to peek out the peephole.

Pulling back, she frowned. It was the plastic surgeon she'd originally scheduled to do the bachelor auction. She opened the door.

"Dr. Ashton. What are you doing here?" Her eyes moved over him. He was short, but stocky. He was bald and wore glasses, and his expression seemed angry.

"Ms. Hightower. I saw the flyers around town. I just got back from a surgical convention in Baltimore, but I thought for sure you would have told me if you'd made this change." He held the flyer up, pointing at the name of the headliner. "I thought I was your headliner. I already told all my patients and colleagues."

"I'm so sorry, Dr. Ashton. It was a last minute change. The opportunity arose and well, he has quite a following. We sold out in a day. I'm sure you understand. For the good of the charity, I had to do what I thought would sell the most tickets."

His chin came up, a sour expression on his face. "Whatever you may have felt you had to do, this was handled badly. It's put me in a bad light with people in the community. Being replaced like that and at the last minute, when plans had already been made. I'll look like the laughing stock."

"Dr. Ashton, I'm sure that's not true."

"Like you care now. You have your Mr. Big Shot tattoo artist. Like any woman would want to date him. I don't even begin to understand the appeal. And now here I am, looking like the town fool."

"Dr. Ashton, it's not like that. But if you'd prefer, I'll make some excuse, like you had some conflicts come up with a speaking engagement or a family wedding or something, and you had to bow out. People would understand."

"It's just that easy for you, isn't it? Just toss aside someone who's helped this charity for years for this *flavor of the month*. Well, if that's how you want to play this, fine. But I'll remember this. And don't count on me for any further donations. I'm done with you and your damn charity!"

With that he stormed off. Ava watched him stalk down the street, and she bit her lip. She hoped he wasn't going to cause her any trouble. She wouldn't have worried too much, except the man was also on the city council with her, and she'd have to see him at every meeting.

Closing the door quietly, she pressed her forehead against it, wondering what else could go wrong in her life.

JAMESON

CHAPTER SEVEN

The next evening at about 6:00, Steffy came strolling in the front door of Brothers Ink. Luckily for Ava, Jameson just happened to be downstairs. She'd worried most of the day on how she was going to arrange that he be around when her sister came in to see her. After all, she couldn't persuade the man to agree to let Steffy replace her if she first didn't put the idea in his head. And she needed him to see Steffy in the tattoo shop for that idea to percolate in his brain. At least, that's how she imagined it would go. He'd see her sweet little sister and realize what a mistake he'd be making if he didn't swap out *Annoying Ava* for *Sweet Steffy*.

Unfortunately, that's not exactly how it went down.

"Hey, Sister," Steffy sang out in her tinkling voice, a melodic feminine sound that had every male head in the place turning to see the pretty blonde walk in.

Ava had to suppress a giggle as she noticed all the O'Rourke brothers craning their necks to get a better look. She stared up at her sister. "Hey, yourself. How'd it go today? Everything run smoothly?"

"No problems at all. I've got it all under control," Steffy answered, her neck straining to try to get a glimpse of the brothers. It didn't take long before Rory was strolling over.

"Did I hear this is your sister?" he asked Ava.

"You did. Rory, this is Stephanie. Steffy, Rory."

He extended his hand. "It's great to meet you. You two work together?"

Stephanie shook his hand. "Usually. Well, except for the time she's been working here."

"I see."

"Are you the one Ava tells me plays in a band?"

"I am. And what else did your sister tell you about me?"

"Just that you were hot as hell," Stephanie admitted brazenly.

That had the man grinning. "Did she now?"

"Steffy!" Ava groaned out.

Jameson approached the counter and glared at Rory. "Don't you have work to do?"

Rory pushed off the counter, gave Stephanie a wink, and sauntered off.

"Something we can do for you?" Jameson asked Ava's sister.

"I, um, just came by to let her know how things went at the office today."

Jameson nodded. "You all caught up now? She needs to get back to work."

Stephanie's eyes moved between Jameson and Ava. "Um, yes, I suppose that was all."

"You don't have to be rude to her," Ava snapped at him.

He pinned her with a piercing look.

Stephanie interrupted before fireworks went off. "That's okay. I'm leaving. No problem."

"Steffy, you don't have to leave," Ava insisted.

"Yes, she does."

"No, she doesn't!"

"Bye, Ava," Stephanie whispered as she made a hasty retreat out the door.

"You're insufferable, you know that? What did she ever do to you?"

"I don't need her in here distracting everyone from their jobs. She did what she came for and left. It's over."

"She sure was gorgeous. Your sister single, Ava?" Liam grinned from his station, knowing it was getting to his brother.

"Little sister is off limits!" Jameson snapped, pointing his finger at Liam.

"You suck the fun out of everything, you know that?"

"What about big sister?" Max asked with a wink at Ava.

"She's off limits, too."

"Figures," Liam grumbled.

"All bets on *that* one are off once you strut down that catwalk, Bro." Max warned Jameson, rubbing it in.

Jameson glared at him.

Max just grinned back. "Just layin' it out there."

When Jameson stalked off, Max strolled over to Ava and leaned down to whisper, "It is so much fun getting him riled up. He hasn't been this riled up since Crystal worked here."

Ava frowned. "Crystal?"

"He had a thing for her. She used to have your job."

"Oh, really? What happened?"

"She left on the back of a bike with an MC patch-holder out of California." When Ava frowned her confusion, Max elaborated. "Member of an MC called the Evil Dead. Some guy she'd been in love with when she lived there. Apparently they'd never gotten over each other. Eventually he came looking for her."

"And Jameson was in love with her?"

"He won't admit it, but he was. We all saw it."

"That must have really torn him up, her leaving like that."

"Yeah. He hasn't really been happy since."

"I see."

CHAPTER EIGHT

The next night at closing time, Ava was alone with Rory. He had one last customer coming in that he'd agreed to stay late for. Jameson had left earlier in the evening, and Max and Liam both had just left. Ava had some new photos that she wanted to upload to the computer files, and she'd offered to stay with him.

"So, this band you're in… do you also write any of the songs?"

"Matter of fact, I just finished one last night. Want to hear it?"

"Yes. I'd love to."

He walked to her desk and pulled a file up on his phone. "I uploaded this last night."

She took in the screen. He was playing the guitar, strumming softly in acoustic. Then he began to sing, and she was struck dumb by how beautiful his voice was. It was a romantic ballad about lost love. She stared up at him, open-mouthed. "Oh my God, Rory. That's amazing. But I thought you were a heavy metal rock band."

"We are. When the guys get a hold of this, they'll speed up the tempo, add a lot of bass and searing guitar solos. You won't recognize it when they get done with it."

She frowned up at him. "But why? It's so beautiful now. Haunting, really. Is that what you want? Them to change it?"

He shrugged. "It doesn't fit the band like this."

"Have you ever thought of going on your own? Perhaps you should keep this one for yourself."

He grinned at her. "Invoking mutiny and anarchy amongst the band, little one?"

"I'm just saying that I like it as it is."

He shrugged. "Maybe. We'll see."

"You're very good."

"Thanks, Ava."

She watched as he walked over and flipped some music on the system. Loud rock pulsed through the room.

"This is Convicted Chrome."

She nodded. They were good. Really good, but still… she hated to think of that lovely love song turned into just another raging heavy-metal dirge.

The door opened and Rory's customer walked in. Rory looked over. "Hey, man."

"Hey, thanks for staying for me. I had a double shift." The man was in hospital scrubs.

"No problem, Aaron. We need to get the shading filled in on that shoulder piece. Hopefully the line work is all healed. Sorry this was the only day I could fit you in. Hate to make you sit for an hour after working all day."

"Hey, sitting will be relaxing after the night I've had. We had a three-car pileup out on the interstate and two heart attacks. The ER was non-stop. I'm looking forward to putting in the ear buds and zoning out to some music."

"Right this way, then. Let's get started." Rory led Aaron back to his station.

Ava got back to work, finishing the photo uploads and organizing the images as best she could. She was also responsible for managing the shop's social media sites and posting shots of some of their latest tattoos. After she finished all that, she took a moment to check her phone for any text messages from Stephanie about work, and then she checked her calendar.

Oh, crap! She frowned down at it. Between juggling her own business and Brothers Ink, she'd completely forgotten a report she had coming up for the next city council meeting. She bit her lip, turning to look at Rory who was just getting started on Aaron's tattoo. She hated to interrupt him, but if she left now, rather than waited until he finished the work which could be more than an hour, she might just have enough time to get home and get the report ready.

Getting up, she walked over to Rory's station.

He glanced up at her. "Need something, sweets?"

"Mind if I take off? I just remembered some work I have to get done tonight."

"Yeah, give me a minute, and I'll walk you out."

"You don't need to do that. I'm parked right out front."

"Ava—"

"Rory, I'll be fine. I promise."

"You're right outside?"

"Yes."

"All right, girl. I'll see you tomorrow."

"Tomorrow." She hurried to her desk, shut down her computer, and grabbed up her purse and jacket. As she hurried out the front door, she called goodbye once more.

Rory glanced up from his customer. "Honk your horn when you get inside your car, so I know you're safe."

She rolled her eyes. "I will."

She hurried out to her car. Climbing inside, she locked the door and tapped the horn. Then she fired it up and pulled out of her spot. It was late and the town was nearly deserted. Shops were long past closed. Even the restaurants were already dark.

She headed down the street and turned the corner. A moment later, a light in her rearview mirror drew her attention. A motorcycle pulled out from an alley, its lone headlight following her down the street at a distance. She continued on, glancing repeatedly in her mirror to keep tabs on the bike. She made another turn and noticed it stuck with her. As she approached her home, she had an uneasy feeling. Turning in the drive, she held her breath as the motorcycle approached, thoughts of the scary biker from the other night filling her head. She let out a sigh of relief as the bike sped past her and roared off down the street.

She was being a paranoid ninny, she thought to herself.

Moving quickly inside, she tossed her bag down and dialed Stephanie. She barely got a greeting out before excited chatter filled her ear.

"Oh my God, Ava! They are all so good looking! I can't believe you hate working there. I'd be looking forward to waking up every morning. Except, well,

Jameson was kind of a jerk."

"Exactly."

"So, I guess from the way he ran me off, the plan for him to swap us out isn't going to happen."

"Guess not. I'll have to think of something else."

"You two have a pretty contentious relationship, huh?"

"Contentious? Are you joking? It's downright combative."

"I suppose," Steffy agreed, and then her voice lit up. "But, oh my God! That Rory was so hot!"

Ava grinned as she replied, "Tonight after work, he played me a song he wrote. Steffy, it was amazing!"

"He writes music, too? That's it, I'm officially in love."

"More like in stalker mode, is what you are."

"Don't tease me! You know how I am about boys in bands."

Ava rolled her eyes. "How could I forget with all the boy band posters you had all over your walls as a child."

"Rory is not boy band material," Stephanie advised her. "He's one hundred percent rock star. There's a big difference."

"Well, he's not a big star yet. But maybe someday

he will be. He's got the talent, that's for sure."

"And right here in Grand Junction."

"Speaking of Grand Junction, I've got a report due for the city council this week. So, I need to get off the phone, sweetie."

"All right. I'll see you in the morning at the office."

"Bye, hon."

Ava disconnected, and then wandered into the living room. She pulled the curtains aside on her front window and peered out, thoughts of that motorcycle filling her head. Seeing nothing, she put it out of her mind and headed to her bedroom. She got out her laptop, sat cross-legged on the bed, and got to work on her report.

CHAPTER NINE

The next evening, Ava was in the break room for her half hour dinner break, talking and laughing with Liam and Max when Jameson stalked in.

"What the hell did you do to the invoice files?"

She slowly pulled the plastic spoon out of her mouth and set the yogurt container down. "Excuse me?"

"The invoice files! Do I have to repeat everything to you?"

She stood, her chair scraping against the linoleum as she stomped to the trashcan and threw the remnants of her dinner away. Then she made to move past him. "If you want an invoice, I'll get it for you. All you have to do is ask. *Nicely.*"

He grabbed her upper arm, halting her. Then his eyes cut to his brothers. "Boys, get out!" Those flashing blue eyes moved back to her. "You, stay!" Chairs scraped across linoleum as the men left them alone. Jameson batted the door with his palm, slamming it shut behind them. Then his attention turned back to her. "I wouldn't need you to get me the damn invoice if you hadn't messed the files all up, so don't act like you're doing me a huge favor."

She tried to pull her arm free, but his grip just tightened. "I merely alphabetized them. I wouldn't think that was so hard to figure out, since it's standard procedure in any office in the country."

"This isn't an office. It's a damn tattoo shop. And I'll keep the files how I want them. Supply vendors up front and utilities and the rest of the crap in the back."

She rolled her eyes. "Why am I not surprised?"

"Think I already told you about rule number one. Don't roll your eyes at me."

"Then get your hands off me." She pulled again, but still he wouldn't let go.

"You don't want to be here any more than I want you here, so let's get one thing straight. This is temporary. I don't need you changing things around while you're here. Got it?"

She jerked her arm free. "Got it."

"Get me the last three months invoices from our insurance provider," he said to her retreating back.

She paused in the doorway. "Health or liability?"

"Liability," he snapped, like it was a stupid question.

She spun on her heels and stalked out.

"Bring them to my office," he yelled after her.

***

Fifteen minutes later she stomped up the stairs with the invoices he'd requested.

"Took you long enough."

"I had a customer to ring up. It took a while to count out his change," she replied snidely letting him know just what she thought of his cash only system.

"Anything else you want to run your mouth about while you're up here?"

"Will that be all?" she bit out.

"No. Sit down." He lifted his chin to one of the chairs in front of his desk.

She plopped down in one.

"What's with the attitude?"

"*My* attitude? *You're* the one with the attitude!"

Jameson glared at her, and then began perusing the invoices, making her sit there waiting while he did so. She began tapping her foot on the hardwood floor.

His eyes snapped up to her. "Quit."

She huffed out a breath, and only when she stopped the tapping did his gaze return to the invoices. He kept her waiting for five long minutes.

Really? How long does it take to scan half a dozen

pages?

When he finally tossed them on the desk and deigned to turn his attention back to her, she'd reached her boiling point.

"I think you and I need to have a little chat," he said.

Oh my God. Now what?

"Sit there while I make a quick phone call, first." Without waiting for a response, he reached for the phone on his desk and punched in a number. He leaned back in his chair, his eyes on her. Someone picked up on the other end and he began speaking.

"Get me Joe Carson, please." He waited a moment. "Joe, this is Jameson O'Rourke." There was a pause. "Still waiting on those corrected invoices. I understand it was a computer error, but it's been three months and they're still coming in wrong." There was another pause. "I've got a short patience for dumbasses and fuckups, and I'm intolerant of slackers. So, which ones you got working for you?" There was another pause. "See that you do."

She watched as he hung up the phone, then his attention returned to her.

"I get you don't want to be here, Ava, any more than I want you here—"

"Then let me find you someone else." She cut him

off.

"You want to let me finish my goddamn sentence?"

She folded her arms, clamping her mouth shut.

"Jesus Christ, Ava. You're the most uptight woman I've ever met."

Her mouth fell open. "I am not!"

"Everything sets you off."

"*Me*? Everything sets *you* off."

"Look at your posture. All defensive."

"Maybe because I feel like you're always attacking me!"

"You need to grow a thicker skin. When I mouth off, you need to let it roll off your back. I wanted the files. You got them. End of story. You don't need to huff and stomp around all night."

"Fine."

He grinned. "Right."

"Was that all?"

His chair creaked as he leaned back, studying her. "No."

Her brow arched. "Something else I can do for you, Mr. O'Rourke."

"Jameson. Think I already set you straight on that at least three times."

"Fine. Jameson."

"I have to cut out early tonight, and Rory's leaving at 8:00."

"All right." She still wasn't sure why he was telling her this.

"It'll just be you, Max, and Liam closing. I know I usually let you go with the last customer, but the guys are staying late to do an inventory supply order, and I wondered if you could stay late and clean up the break room and sweep the shop."

She knew those were jobs that the men usually did, and she was leery of staying late because of her encounter with that scary biker the other night. She bit her lip.

At her hesitation, his eyes narrowed on her. "You got a problem with that?"

The last thing she wanted to do was tell him about her silly fears. She didn't want to give him another excuse to think she was being difficult. So, instead of mentioning it, she replied, "Of course not. Whatever you need."

"Means you may not get out of here till late."

"I'll manage."

"Great." He stroked his beard.

"Is that all?"

"That's all, Ms. Hightower."

She wanted to correct him, but she'd be damned if she'd sit here and watch the smirk on his face. She stood and headed toward the stairs, but stopped short, turning back. "Let me know when you're through with the invoices, and I'll re-file them."

She caught his eyes on her ass. They flicked up to hers quick enough, but she'd seen. Evidently the man wasn't as immune to the tight skirts she wore as he pretended to be.

An idea formed in her head. Tomorrow she'd wear jeans, just to see if he noticed.

CHAPTER TEN

Ava came in about quarter to 11:00 the next morning. The front door was unlocked, but the closed sign was still flipped. She set her purse on her chair and glanced around. The lights were on, but the place looked deserted.

"Max? Liam?" Getting no response, she wandered toward the rear of the shop and peered in the break room. It was empty as well.

She jogged up the open staircase to the second floor loft that Jameson used for his office, calling his name as she climbed the steps. "Jameson, you up here?"

Getting no answer and finding it empty, she turned and headed downstairs. Where could they all be? Going down the back hall, she peered in the clean room where they sterilized equipment and then the storage room where they kept supplies. Nada.

She opened the door to the piercing room, thinking one of them might be in there restocking. It was empty.

Finally, she opened the door to the private room they used for tattooing intimate areas of the body. Not really expecting to find a customer inside since it was before hours, she didn't bother to knock. Peering in, she saw Jameson bent over a female body, his tattoo machine in hand, the needle applying ink to the side of a woman's bare breast. She was turned away, but her back was bared, and it was obvious she was topless on the table she reclined on.

His head swiveled at the sound of the door opening, and the woman gasped, jolting to cover herself. Jameson had just enough time to pull the needle from her skin as she scrambled to cross her arms over herself, crying, "Oh my God."

Jameson moved in front of her, shielding her from Ava's sight and snapped, "Get out!"

Ava was so shocked, not only by the customer inside, but also by the fact that the woman had been topless and Jameson had been inking her breast. Ava dashed back up to her desk.

Liam was just coming in, pulling the strap of his messenger bag over his head and setting it on the floor at his station. He kept large sketchpads inside, filled with art that came to him at all hours. He frowned when he saw the expression on her face. "You okay, Ava?"

She shook her head. "Oh, my God. I just walked in

on Jameson and a customer. He's back there tattooing some chick's boob. Talk about mortified. I had no idea anyone was in the shop. We're not even open yet."

Liam's eyes slid past her toward the private room and his expression changed. "Fuck, I forgot about the appointment Jamie set up. I should have warned you."

Ava frowned. "What do you mean?

"I was here when he had the initial consultation with her. The woman is a breast cancer survivor. She went through reconstruction, but wanted to see about getting some ink to cover the scars on the sides of her breasts."

Ava felt like crawling under the desk. "Oh, my God. I can't believe I walked in on them. She was probably so embarrassed. I mean, I didn't see anything, but now I see why she was so freaked out when I peeked inside."

She put her face in her hands.

"You didn't mean to do it. I should have warned you. Hell, Jameson should have warned you."

"He's told me never to walk in the private rooms without knocking. The look on his face… He wanted to kill me."

"Hey, doll, we all make mistakes. Don't beat yourself up about it. Just apologize to the lady when she comes out."

"Maybe I should make myself scarce, so she doesn't have to look at me."

"Don't blow it out of proportion."

"You didn't see the look on Jameson's face."

***

An hour later, with the shop now open and customers in Max, Liam, and Rory's chairs, Jameson walked his customer to the front. She put her purse on the counter, but wouldn't look at Ava as she dug for her wallet.

"I'm so sorry about earlier, ma'am. I didn't realize there were any customers in the shop."

The woman just waved her away, but still wouldn't look at her and had a cold expression on her face. "Don't worry about it."

Ava watched as she dug out a stack of bills and dropped them on the counter. "I don't need the change."

Jameson walked her to the door.

Ava watched their exchange as he laid his hand on her shoulder, and leaned in to speak to her in a hushed tone. She nodded, a small smile pulling at her mouth, and then left with her head down.

Jameson shut the door and turned, his eyes drilling

into Ava's. "Don't ever make that mistake again."

She tried to explain. "I didn't know. I'm sorry, I—"

He stalked away with no regard for her apology.

***

Jameson stayed up in his office for a few hours before leaving that afternoon, still in a mood. Ava's eyes followed him as he walked over to tell Liam he was cutting out. She noticed Liam's eyes drop past Jamie to connect with hers as he told him, "No problem. We've got it covered."

Jameson didn't turn to look at her.

After he walked away, she felt her eyes sting with tears. Knowing she'd messed up so badly was tearing her apart. She turned quickly away, but Liam saw.

A few minutes later, after they heard Jameson's bike roar off, she looked up to find Liam leaning his forearms on the upper counter of her reception desk.

"You okay, doll?"

She tried to smile. "I'm fine."

Liam turned his head, his eyes gazing out the front window. Then he pushed off the counter, rapped on it twice with his knuckles, and walked away.

She busied herself with checking inventory and placing orders for things they were low on. The whole time, her mind was going over and over just how big she'd screwed up and how awful that woman must have felt. Worst of all, it had reflected poorly on Jameson. He had a reputation, and she'd quite possibly, albeit unwittingly, damaged it. Word of mouth and bad reviews could irreparably damage a business, no matter how big a name you had.

She bit her lip. Somehow she had to make this right, but how? The only thing she could think to do was try to apologize again to Jameson, and perhaps send the woman a heartfelt apology note as well.

The time rolled around when they all took turns taking dinner breaks, and Ava wandered over to Liam's station. He was just cleaning up from his last customer.

"Are you going to be taking a dinner break now?" she asked quietly.

"I was thinking about it. You want to join me, sweets?" He glanced toward the reception waiting area. There were no customers waiting and none scheduled for him for the next hour and a half.

"Actually, I was wondering if you knew if Jameson was home. I'd like to go speak to him, try to apologize again."

"I see." He studied her. "Yeah, he said he was going home."

"Could you tell me how to get out there? I know it's southeast of town somewhere."

"I can do better than that. I can take you there myself. That is if you're up for a ride. I've got my bike outside."

"You'd do that for me?"

"You bet."

She glanced over her shoulder to where Max was putting a stencil to a man's arm. "It'd be okay? We'd be back soon?"

Max, who must have heard the entire conversation, looked up. "I got it covered, babe. I'm a multi-tasker."

"See, problem solved." Liam grinned down at her.

"All right. If you don't mind."

"Not at all."

"I've never ridden before," she warned.

He waggled his brows. "So I get to pop your cherry?"

She turned five shades of red. "Oh, my God. Shut up."

He chuckled and led her out to his bike.

***

Twenty minutes later, they were rolling down a dirt and gravel driveway to an old farmhouse set back from the road. There was a large three-car garage behind the house. The big doors were open, and they could see the shadowed silhouette of Jameson inside working on an old vintage red car. He turned when he heard them roll up.

Ava climbed from the bike as Liam shut it off and dropped the kickstand.

He paused, his eyes moving from her to the garage. Then he lifted his chin toward it. "He's working on his '63 Mercury Comet, his prized possession. He works on it whenever he's pissed off about something. It calms him down. Go on. I'm heading inside to make a sandwich." He paused to wink at her. "He runs you off, come inside and I'll make you one."

She nodded.

Liam moved toward the house, and her eyes shifted to the garage. She stood rooted to the spot, unsure how Jameson would receive her. Taking a deep breath, she gathered her courage and headed toward him.

As she came into the dim garage, it took her eyes a moment to adjust to the darkness. When they did, she realized he was shirtless. Her eyes slid over him; he was covered in colorful ink. *Covered*. Normally, she would have found it unattractive, but on him, it worked. Holy hell, did it work. She couldn't take her eyes off of him. That is, until he barked at her.

"What are you doing here?"

"I—"

"Shouldn't you be at the shop?"

"It's my dinner break."

"And you're here why?"

"Liam brought me out."

"I saw who brought you out. What I want to know is why?"

He was being a bear. She'd half expected this. Lifting her chin, she mustered the courage to swallow her pride and say what she'd come to tell him. "This morning, when I walked in on you… I'm sorry. I had no idea we had customers in the shop. The door had been unlocked, the lights were on, but I couldn't find anyone."

"So you barged into a private room."

"I'm not trying to make excuses. I'm so sorry. I never would want to embarrass a customer, especially—"

"Especially, what?"

"Liam told me about the appointment. I mean, afterward. Not before."

Jameson picked up a pack of cigarettes and shook one out, then dug in his hip pocket, coming up with a lighter. Flicking it on, the flame arced high, illuminating his face as he dipped his head, drawing on his cigarette until it flared to life. His eyes pierced into hers like blue lasers the entire time.

"That's bad for you, you know," she murmured.

He blew a plume of smoke out with a glare, and she could feel the anger radiating off him from across the six feet that separated them.

"That it?"

She could see he wasn't going to make this easy. She felt bad, but he was not being very receptive of her apology. "I just wanted you to know how sorry I am. And I'll send the woman a note telling her the same."

He sucked another deep drag off his cigarette, his eyes drilling into hers. "Save it. She wouldn't be happy to have you track her down. She wanted privacy. Anonymity. Not half the shop knowing she was there or the reason why. That hard for you to understand?"

"No, of course not. I—"

"Just wanted to apologize. Right. Well, you've done that. Now go." He lifted his chin toward the house.

She dropped her head and stepped back, then walked to the house. She couldn't make him accept her apology; she could only offer it.

***

Jameson watched her go. He'd treated her like shit, he knew that, and part of that was a defense mechanism. When her eyes had dropped to his chest, and her pupils had dilated—her eyes wide as she'd gazed at him, her lips parting as she'd inhaled sharply—he couldn't deny it had affected him. The sound had made his dick hard, pressing against the zipper of his jeans, and all he could think about was sliding his hands underneath that curvy ass of hers, placing her smack dab on the hood of the car, and fucking her right there and then. He'd noticed the jeans she wore today, faded denim that hugged her body from hip to knee. They looked good on her. Damn good.

What the hell was wrong with him? Seems lately, screwing her was all he could think about. His eyes dropped, and he watched her hips sway as she walked away. Then he sent the cigarette arcing into the air and turned back to take out his frustration on the metal of the car frame.

CHAPTER ELEVEN

Two days later, Ava was at the counter, Max was working on a client, Liam was on dinner break, and Rory, who was late getting back from an out of town gig, hadn't made it in yet. A young girl walked in the door dressed in a dark hoodie that was pulled over her head. Bright pink hair peeked out the side. She was thin and frail with pale skin and big eyes. She had a timid way about her as she approached the counter.

Ava tried to put her at ease with a big smile. "Hi, welcome to Brothers Ink. Are you here for an appointment?"

The girl nodded, and then slowly pushed the hood back, saying quietly, "I have an appointment with Rory at 5:00 p.m."

Ava pulled the calendar up on the computer. Sure enough, there was the appointment. Knowing Rory wasn't in the shop, she stalled for time, having the girl fill out the necessary paperwork and checking her ID, all the while trying to come up with what to tell her. She finally smiled up at the girl, "If you'll please have a seat, I'll see if he's ready for you."

As the girl sat down, Ava walked back through the tattoo stations. She could see that Max was nowhere near finished with his client, so she headed up the stairs to Jameson's office. She entered the loft and moved toward his desk. He stood with his back to her, staring out the window. His cell phone was in his hand and the call was on speaker. He glanced over his shoulder at her approach, but continued with his conversation. She stood quietly waiting for him to finish.

"Thought you were coming straight here when you got back to town," Jameson said.

The reply came over the speaker, and Ava recognized it immediately as Rory's voice.

"Nah, we got a late start. Won't make it back for a couple of hours."

Jameson shook his head. "Why didn't you say so?"

"Thought you knew, Bro."

"Sorry, I let the guy I pay to tail your every move and keep me informed have the day off. Something at his kid's school, I think," Jameson said, sarcastically and Ava fought to hold back a smile.

"You're hilarious. Ha ha," came Rory's response.

Jameson's brows shot up. "What I am is pissed."

"Be there as soon as I can."

JAMESON

Jameson tossed the phone on the desk, his eyes connecting with hers. "What can I do for you?"

"Um, there's a girl here for Rory. She has a 5:00 with him. He's not even close, is he?"

"Nope. He's still two hours out." He slid his hands into his pockets.

"Okay. Should I try to reschedule her then?"

Jameson glanced at his watch, twisting his wrist to see the face. "No. Let me see what she wants. Maybe I can do it for her."

He followed her down to the lobby. Ava moved behind the desk, and Jameson approached the only girl waiting. He extended his hand.

"Hi, I'm Jameson, Rory's brother. I understand you have an appointment with him."

Her eyes moved from Jameson to Ava as she shook his hand. "Yes. Is he here?"

"I'm afraid he's running late driving back from Denver. But I'd be happy to take the appointment if you're okay with it. I'm pretty good."

She glanced up at the magazine covers framed on the wall. "Um, yes I know, it's just, Rory knew what I wanted and—"

"How about you come on back, and we'll go over what you want? I'll sketch something out, and if you don't like it, you can reschedule with Rory?"

"Well, um…I suppose that would be all right."

Jameson led the girl back to a station.

Ava watched out of the corner of her eye as he helped the girl into the chair, and then rolled a stool over to her. Ava couldn't hear their conversation, but she watched, fascinated at how gentle Jameson was with the timid girl. He listened intently to her, smiling and chatting and trying to put her at ease. Finally, after some discussion between them, Ava saw the girl slowly pull the sleeves of her hoodie up, revealing her wrists.

Jameson stared down at them a long moment, and then he reached up, taking one in his hand and tenderly brushing his thumb across the inside, just above her palm. Ava could tell even from a distance that something deep and important was transpiring between them. She frowned, wondering what tattoo the girl was getting. Perhaps it was in memory of a loved one whom she'd lost.

Ava thought it was always sad when people came in for tattoos honoring someone's memory. Whenever the ink was finished, they were usually in tears looking at it and all it represented.

An hour or so later, Jameson walked the girl up to the counter. When the girl reached into her pocket and pulled out some bills, Jameson waved her off, refusing the payment. Then he escorted her to the door. He murmured something quietly, and hugged her. She smiled and nodded at something he said, and then turned and left.

Ava looked away when he turned back, not wanting to appear to be watching, but as Jameson strode past her desk, he snapped, "When Rory gets in, tell him I want to fucking see him!"

She stared wide-eyed after him as he stalked off. What had caused the sudden change? One minute he was soft and tender toward the young girl, the next he was pissed as all hell. She dropped her eyes from Jameson's retreating back and connected with Max's gaze. He stared knowingly into hers, but said nothing, then returned his attention to his customer.

An hour later, Rory made it in. He glanced toward Ava with a greeting and a smile.

"Hey, sweets."

She stopped him as he passed. "Rory, Jameson wants to see you."

He paused, frowning.

"You missed your 5:00 appointment." Ava looked down at the release the girl had filled out. "A girl named Mariah. Jameson took the appointment for you."

Rory's eyes slid closed. "Shit."

Ava studied him. "He seemed a little upset."

He nodded. "Yeah. I better go talk to him."

She watched him stop to talk quietly with Max. They exchanged a few hushed but heated words. Ava frowned, wondering what in the world it was all about.

Liam was just finishing with the last customer in the shop, and he walked the man up to the counter to pay. It distracted her from the drama going on around them. When she'd collected the money and the customer had left, she could hear the sounds of a muffled argument drifting down the stairway from Jameson's office. She couldn't make out the words but could hear the raised voices. She caught Max's eyes, and he walked over to her.

"Don't worry about it, sweetheart. They'll work it out."

"Work what out? Why is Jameson so upset?"

Max leaned his forearms down on the counter, rubbing his palms together. "The tattoo Jamie did for that girl, the one he had to take because Rory wasn't here?"

"Yes, what about it? He seemed really good with her, and she seemed pleased with the work he'd done. I mean, I didn't actually see what it looked like, but—"

"I'm sure she was happy with the work. That's not the problem."

"What, then? He was mad he had to cover for Rory and take his appointment?"

"It wasn't that he had to take Rory's appointment; it was the type of tattoo the girl asked for. He just wasn't prepared for that."

She frowned. "A wrist tattoo? Aren't those pretty common?"

"She was getting it to cover some scars."

"Okay. So? That's not all that uncommon, is it?"

"No. Not saying it is. But these…"

"It didn't bother him to tattoo that other woman's scar. Why is this so different?"

"Because the scars she wanted covered were marks from where she'd attempted suicide."

"Oh, my God."

"Yeah."

"And that's why he was upset?"

"Well, she isn't the first girl who's had scars like that. I think it brought back some bad memories for him. Remember I told you about Crystal, the receptionist we used to have?"

"Yes."

"She was the last one he'd tattooed scars like that for."

"Really? She'd tried to kill herself?"

"That stuff happened before she started working here. She hid the scars under bracelets for the longest time. Finally, Jameson got her to talk about it. I think it was one of the things that drew them together, her opening up to him like that, trusting him enough to share that story with him."

"I see. That must have been difficult for her."

"Yeah. Anyway, he hasn't tattooed anyone with scars like hers since then. He avoids them. Too painful, I guess. So, you see, taking that appointment, not realizing what kind of tattoo that girl was going to want, he wasn't prepared, and I'm sure it hit him hard."

"He was so good with the girl. I mean, the way he treated her."

"Yeah, Jamie has a way with customers, especially women, especially nervous ones. I know maybe you haven't seen him do many tattoos, but he has a way of making them feel at ease. He talks them through it, distracting them from their fear."

She looked toward the staircase. She felt bad he'd been shoved into that appointment without being prepared for what he was walking into. She could understand why he'd be upset with Rory. But, more than anything, she admired the way he'd handled the girl, never letting her see the anger or that it had hit so close to home for him. And then not taking her money, and that moment at the door, the way he'd hugged her, and gotten a smile from her…

She realized she was starting to see a whole new side to the man.

CHAPTER TWELVE

Jameson eyed the plastic collection jar on the counter. It was midafternoon, and he finally had time to come down from his office; he'd spent the entire morning catching up on bills and going over bank statements. "What the hell is that?"

Liam swiveled it around so Jameson could see the handwritten label.

Cuss Jar.

"It's Ava's," Liam explained.

"What the fuck is a Cuss Jar?"

"You swear, you gotta put a buck in the jar. It's for charity. Since you walked up, you've cussed twice, so ante up two bucks, Jamie."

"Are you shittin' me? You guys going along with this?"

"Yup. And now you owe three."

Jameson dug in his pocket and pulled out a twenty. "Here, I'm sure I'll use that before the night's over." He watched as a huge grin split Ava's face. Then he rolled his eyes and stalked off.

She called after his retreating back. "Hey, how come you can roll your eyes and I can't?"

"Because I'm the boss and you're not. And don't you forget it, sweetheart."

"Don't call me that!" she yelled after him.

His voice echoed down the stairs. "Too late, I already did."

Max and Liam both chuckled at their bickering and sauntered back to their stations.

***

A couple hours later, Rory came in the front door. He peered into the tip jar loaded with bills. "Whoa! Who put the twenty in?"

"Jameson. He's paying ahead for the night."

Rory chuckled. "How much credit does he have left?"

Ava tilted her head to the side, eyeing the ceiling as she considered. "Hmm. He's got about three bucks left."

Rory burst out laughing. "Your poor virgin ears."

She rolled her eyes. "I'll survive."

"No doubt." He eyed the jar. "Your charity is really cleaning up, huh?"

"That it is." She slid the jar toward him. "Care to contribute?"

He dug in his pocket and pulled out a five. "Let me know when this runs out."

She giggled. "Oh, you can count on it."

He slapped the counter, winked at her, and walked off.

***

Ava was in the break room halfway through her dinner break when she heard angry raised voices coming from the front of the shop. Frowning, she got up and peered out the door.

There was definitely arguing coming from the lobby. She walked cautiously up, standing in the background only to observe Jameson dividing his attention between Rory and some girl.

Ava's eyes swept over the girl, taking her in from head to toe. She looked like a groupie. Her jeans rode low on her hip, her red hair hung in tangles down her back. Her makeup was heavily applied, and she looked strung out on something.

Jameson got right in her face.

"Sweetheart, look in my fucking eyes and hear what I'm saying. The last thing my brother is doing is going back to Utah with you. I don't care how fucking fantastic a time you think you had with him or how rich your daddy is. Understand?"

She put her hands on her hips and stared over at Rory. "Rory, are you coming or not?"

"Not," Jameson bit out. "Now get the fuck out."

"Fine!" She stomped toward the door, flung it open, and turned to glare at Rory.

He made a move to go after her, but Jameson put a hand in his chest, pushing him back. "Don't even think about it."

She stormed off, and Jameson turned back to Rory. "She's nothing but a fucking druggie and a gold digger. Thinks she's going to hitch her crazy train to you hoping you'll hit the big time. She ain't worth it, Rory. She'll only drag you down."

Rory shoved Jameson's hand away, but kept his mouth shut and stormed back to the break room.

Jameson called after him, "I hope to hell you wore a goddamn condom."

Rory flipped him off and kept walking.

Ava watched Rory go as he passed her, and then she turned back to Jameson. She saw the truth. Yes, the girl was probably a bad influence Rory didn't need in his life, but that wasn't what scared Jameson the most. Ava would bet her next paycheck on it. What Jameson was really afraid of was that she'd pull his brother away and break up his family.

"Jameson, you can't decide that for him—"

He whirled, pointing a finger at her. "You try and come between me and my brothers and I'll show you the door as well, sweet-cheeks, and your Gala be damned."

She'd put up with his temper long enough, and suddenly she had the backbone to finally tell him off.

"You can't control everyone!"

"Stay out of this. And don't tell me what I can and can't do. I'm your boss, or have you forgotten that?"

"How could I? You won't *let* me forget. I've tried everything I can to please you and can't. Nothing I do is good enough for you, is it? *Is it?*"

He frowned at the sudden turn the argument had taken. "Calm the fuck down, Ava."

"Don't tell me to calm down. And don't swear at me."

"Christ, woman. You'd try the patience of a saint."

"Jamie, enough!" Max barked.

Ava began to tear up.

"Babe, come here," Jameson said in a quiet, but stern voice.

"No."

Disregarding her reply, he moved toward her, his hand clamped around her wrist, and he pulled her behind him toward the back. He dragged her down the hall and into the storeroom. His free hand came up to bat the door shut with a bang.

She yanked her hand free, and he released it. She wiped the tears off her cheek, anger replacing the hurt.

Running a hand through his hair, he blew out a breath. "I didn't mean to snap at you, Ava. But what goes on in this shop between my brothers and me is none of your business. You're here to work the front counter, that's it, and only temporarily at that. Got it?"

"Got it," she snapped back. "Can I go now?"

"No." He jammed his hands on his hips, staring at her, and she watched as he appeared to struggle to control his emotions. "You want out of this deal?"

She lifted her chin. "Not on your life."

"Why can't you admit this is a shit deal for both of us and cut your losses?"

"It's not a shit deal. The Gala is important to me. I thought those parking spots were important to you."

"You're not going to last till then."

"Yes, I am. I have to."

They stared each other down, and she watched his eyes drop to her mouth. For a moment all the sparks flying between them, and the small room they were in that barely allowed more than a foot between them, became all too apparent to her. And she could see by the way he was looking at her that he felt it as well. Suddenly, all she could hear was his heavy breathing, and her eyes dropped to watch his chest move in and out. Still they were quiet, neither speaking, as if they were caught in a spell neither of them wanted to be the one to break.

Finally, she lifted her eyes to see his burning into hers. His hands came up to grab her face, his fingers sliding into the hair behind her ears as he pulled her close. She watched his eyes drop to her mouth for a long moment, and she was sure he was going to kiss her, but then just as suddenly, he released her and opened the door, storming out and leaving her standing there unsure what had just happened.

She walked out and quietly shut the door as the sound of Jameson's boots pounding up the stairs to his office carried to her. She walked back up front. There were no customers, and Rory was sitting on one of the couches, staring at the floor. Max was leaning against the counter and Liam stood with his boots spread and his arms folded.

Rory looked up when she returned. "You okay, doll?"

She nodded and asked quietly, "Are you okay?"

A smile tugged at the corner of his mouth, and he huffed out a breath. "He's right about the girl, and maybe I saw it."

"But that's your decision. Not his," Ava argued.

"Maybe if you stick around, you'll help him see that," Liam put in.

Ava looked over at him. "Me? I can't get him to see anything."

"Bullshit," Liam replied.

She arched a brow at him and glanced at the cuss jar.

He rolled his eyes, slid his hand in his hip pocket, pulled out a bill, and shoved it in the jar. Then continued, "He's changing, Ava. Maybe you can't see it, but we all can. And you're the reason for that change."

Max and Rory both nodded when she glanced to see if they agreed with Liam. She shook her head, not believing that for a second. "You're all crazy."

"Not seeing it, doesn't make it not so," Max stated.

She grinned. "More prophetic words from Maxwell O'Rourke?"

"Exactly." He grinned, tousled her hair, and then pulled her in for a quick bear hug.

"Want to know my theory?" Liam asked.

"Do tell," Ava replied, laughing in Max's hold, but giving Liam her attention.

Liam's brows lifted as he stared into her eyes and challenged, "I think you two like fighting, or maybe you're both just scared of what would happen if you stop."

The smile on Ava's face faded as his words sunk in. Were they true? What *would* happen if they stopped fighting each other over everything?

CHAPTER THIRTEEN

Ava sat at her kitchen table, staring out the window. She felt like she was failing again. For most of her life, failure was foreign to her. She'd always done well in school, always been little Miss Perfect obtaining straight A's. When she'd first set up her business, she'd studied everything she could to be sure it was a success. Her type-A personality wouldn't let her do anything less. She'd always felt so in control of her life. At least she had until her sister had gotten ill. Then she'd felt completely out of control. She'd tried so hard to get her sister well, to get her all the medical attention she could, taking her to doctor after doctor, chasing after a cure for a disease that soon ravaged her poor younger sibling. Having lost her mother and father in the years just before Lily was diagnosed, the responsibility for her care had all fallen to Ava, the oldest.

She'd taken on the task with no hesitation. But with it, came her first failure, and it had been a big one. She'd been unable to save her baby sister, no matter how hard they both fought.

Now it seemed she was letting down the charity she'd created in her memory. She was about to lose this bet and with it, her biggest draw for the Gala. She hung her head. It was so hard to swallow, and it felt like she was letting her sister down all over again.

If only Jameson would see she just wanted to help. She wasn't trying to attack him, but nothing she did was right in his eyes—he only seemed to see her as the enemy.

She thought back to the conversation she'd had with Max the day he'd taken her for ice cream. It had been quite a revelation into the inner psyche of the town's golden boy. He wasn't at all what she'd thought; he was fighting for his family. It seemed he'd always been fighting for his family, and that was something she could admire and relate to wholeheartedly. It touched something in her—made her want to fight *for* him, not against him.

She sat up straighter, an idea taking shape in her brain. Perhaps that was the key to all of this. Perhaps if she showed him she wanted to help him, truly help him, he'd stop seeing it as an attack. Maybe, just maybe, they could find some common ground.

Perhaps if he felt her true desire to help, he in turn

would go along with helping with the Gala, not grudgingly, but enthusiastically.

Her eyes darted over the table. The only problem was she knew next to nothing about his industry, and if she really wanted to help him, she was going to have to change that. Researching and learning about a topic was nothing foreign to her, and now that she had a plan, it made tackling the challenge that much easier. She grabbed a notepad, flipped open her laptop, and got to work.

CHAPTER FOURTEEN

After closing time, Ava found the guys all sitting in the break room drinking beer. Max looked up when he saw her walk in, and he held up his bottle. "Can I get you one, Ava?"

"Yeah, come join us, sweetie," Rory added.

Liam slid the chair next to him, patting the seat in invitation.

She smiled, her eyes moving around the group of four men. "No thanks on the beer, but there is something I wanted to talk about, if you don't mind."

Jameson leaned back in his seat, his arms folded. "Okay, shoot."

Ava cleared her throat and glanced down at some of the information she'd printed off last night. "I know I don't know anything about your business, but despite what you think, I really do want to help you." She looked right at Jameson when she said it. "So, I did a little research last night. By little, meaning I was up until 2:00 a.m."

"You don't need to do that, Ava," Jameson said

softly.

She met his eyes. "I want to contribute. I think I can."

"This is only temporary," he reminded her.

"Hear her out, Jamie," Max put in, turning to his brother and then nodding at her. "Go on, Ava."

"I have some ideas here that may help."

"Help what?" Jameson snapped.

"I know until a few short years ago there really weren't any software programs specifically developed for tattoo and piercing shop management, so I'm sure when you started this business, there wasn't anything available. And I understand that change can be daunting. The expression 'why fix it if it's not broke' comes to mind. But I think if you take a look at some of the programs I've found, you'll see the benefits can be substantial and help grow the business." She passed out copies of the bullet points.

"Not just by simplifying the processes, but they can help you operate the shop as efficiently, effectively, and profitably as possible.

"They have tools that can help you stay on top of client data, inventory, artists' schedules, just to name a few.

"There are features for appointment management

that help monitor your schedules. You can even schedule appointments that will sync with your calendars, send clients automated text messages and email reminders as well as notify each of you when a client cancels. They'll even allow you to manage your schedules from your mobile devices.

"There are tools that allow your clients to sign paperless release forms and receive aftercare instructions electronically. You can also keep track of the products clients buy for marketing purposes and which services each client receives. And as a bonus, all the client data you store in the program can easily be exported for health inspectors to review when necessary.

"The program also has point of sale capabilities that allow you to charge client's credit cards, print receipts, sell gift cards and more.

"Then there's inventory management. It can keep track of stock levels so you know when you need to re-order, and you'll never run out of a product that's critical to your business again.

"There are a variety of reporting functions that can track what marketing is working and what isn't, view customer demographics and more. You can even run scenarios to see how much more or less you'd make if you charged hourly vs. by tattoo size.

"And lastly, if you were to ever own more than one shop, you can connect locations, and it will allow you to access data from a single database no matter where you are. You can share customer information and gift card balances between shops. If a client wants a product you're out of at one shop, you can quickly check to see if you have it at another location."

"That it? You done?" Jameson asked, seemingly not impressed or interested in any of it.

Ava lifted her chin. "You don't agree that some of these ideas are worth at least exploring?"

Jameson obviously didn't, he just stared back at her, uninterested.

"I do," Max said.

"Me, too," Liam agreed.

Rory looked over at Jameson. "Why haven't we done any of this before?"

Jameson answered him, but his eyes remained drilled into Ava's. "Because all this fancy shit costs money. Big money. We're doing fine."

"You just can't admit that someone else may have a better way of doing things. I'm trying to help you." Ava held his eyes.

"You're meddling in things that don't concern you.

Goddamn, woman. You're a pain in my ass."

Her composure snapped. "And you're a stubborn jerk with control issues."

"Well, that's the pot calling the kettle black, now isn't it?" Jameson bit right back.

"I do not have control issues."

"Right."

"Are you saying these ideas hold no merit?" She cocked a brow at him, challenging.

He clamped his jaw tight and asked through his teeth, "Is that all, Ms. Hightower?"

"Yes, Mr. O'Rourke, that's all. I don't know why I would expect you to listen to the only person in here who actually has business training." Fuming, she tossed her material on the table and stalked out.

***

The brothers all turned to stare at Jameson.

"Goddamn, she's as obstinate as she is hot," he snarled. "But hell, I've never met a woman yet who didn't try to make things more complicated than they needed to be. Why should she be any different, right?" He paused to look at his brothers, who sat staring at him with their arms crossed.

"You're a fool," Liam finally pronounced.

"Why do you have to be such an ass?" Max asked

bluntly.

"What?" Jameson replied. "You want to pay for that shit she was talking about out of *your* pocket, Max? Be my guest."

"Jamie—"

"You seriously want to change everything we do? Learn a whole new fucking system?" He glared. "Why the hell do women always think they have to change things?"

Max stared him down. "She's changed a few things, yeah, but for the better. Ain't one of those changes weren't a huge improvement, same with all these suggestions. You just can't stand it cause it's not *your* way. You can't admit her way is better."

Liam shifted the toothpick in his mouth. "Why don't you ease off on her? No reason this has to be such a fucked up situation. She's good. Damn good. Treat that as a gift, not a fucking problem."

"Jamie doesn't want to uphold his end of the bargain, and he plans to make sure he doesn't have to… even if that means playin' dirty," Max informed Liam, his eyes drilling into Jameson. "Isn't that right?"

Liam's gaze swung to Max, and then narrowed on his oldest brother. "That true, Bro? That's a fucking shitty thing to do."

Rory let the front legs of his tipped back chair fall to the floor with a bang. "Wait a minute. What bargain?"

Jameson tilted his beer bottle toward Max, ignoring Rory. "You got me into this mess. Thought you were so fucking funny signing that damned release."

Max huffed out a breath. "Look, Jamie. Okay, you're right. I may hold some blame—"

"*Some?*"

"You want to let me finish?"

Jameson clamped his mouth shut and silently fumed.

"I'll make you a deal. You ease up on her, and I'll walk the damn runway with you."

"What the hell are you guys talking about? Walk what runway?" Rory demanded.

Liam chucked. "You haven't seen the flyers? They're up all over town. Big brother is Grand Junction's most eligible bachelor. So eligible, in fact, that he's being auctioned off for charity."

"The hell I am," Jamie snapped.

Rory burst out laughing. "You're shittin' me."

"Nope. He's the main attraction."

"Fuck that," Jameson grumbled, finishing off his beer.

Max stood up. "Come on, Jamie, if you do it, I'll do it."

Jameson glared up at him. "Oh, believe me, if I have to do it, you are definitely gonna do it. You'll be right up there with me, *Brother*."

Max extended his hand. "Fine. You ease up on Ava, deal?"

Jameson grudgingly stood and shook his hand, but qualified it. "Easing up doesn't mean I'm gonna be a fucking pushover."

The brothers watched as he threw his bottle in the trash and stalked out.

Max slid his hands in his pockets. "Five bucks says he's gonna turn into a marshmallow before this is through."

The men snorted, trying to hold in their laughter.

***

Two days later, Ava walked into the break room to get a cup of coffee. Jameson appeared to be fixing the small piece of countertop on the side cabinet that needed replacing. He had a new piece on the floor, and he was marking it with a carpentry pencil where he needed to cut it.

Ava glanced from the replacement piece to the cabinet and back again. It seemed obvious to her that he was cutting it too small.

"Are you sure you want to cut it there?"

He gave her a look of death over his shoulder. "I know what I'm doing, Ava."

"It looks too small."

"I measured it." He turned back to what he was doing.

"You're sure?"

"Yes, *Little Miss Fix-it*, I'm sure. You want to make a bet?"

She folded her arms, thrusting her hip out. "Okay, boss man. Five bucks says you cut it too small."

"Fine. Five bucks. Now get back to work and let me finish up without you bothering me."

She marched up front.

Twenty minutes later, Jameson walked around to the front of the counter, stretched up, and nailed a $5 bill to the wall high above her station, well out of her reach.

Then he turned, glared, and stalked off.

His brothers came to stand by her station. She leaned back in her chair, her arms folded. They all stared up at the bill.

"Want me to pull the nail out for you and get it down?" Max offered.

She grinned. "Nope. I think I'm going to leave it there to remind myself how sweet this moment is — the moment Jameson had to admit he's not always right."

They all burst out laughing.

Liam held his hand out and high-fived her. "Touché, darlin'."

CHAPTER FIFTEEN

Jameson walked past the piercing room and heard voices coming from the open door. He paused, leaning against the doorframe with his arms folded.

Rory, who did most of the piercings for the shop, was holding up a piece of Prince Albert Jewelry in front of Ava's face, and she looked white as a sheet, or maybe a little green around the gills.

"What the fuck are you doing?" Jameson snapped.

Rory turned to look at him. They both did.

"Showing Ava our line of jewelry."

"What the fuck for?"

"She's got to know what customers are asking about when they come in."

"No, she fucking doesn't. She books an appointment or refers them to one of us. She does not need a fucking lesson in genital jewelry."

He watched the corner of his brother's mouth pull up. "You say so, boss."

Jameson jerked his head toward the front of the shop, his eyes drilling into Rory's. "Get back to work."

Rory put the piece of jewelry back, winked at Ava, and strolled out, making sure to bump shoulders with Jameson as he passed through the doorway.

Ava looked nervously toward Jameson and made to move past him, but he stepped in front of her, blocking her way. He wasn't even sure why he did it, but he didn't want her to go. Not yet.

"You got questions?" he bit out.

Her lips parted breathlessly. "What?"

He reached behind him and closed the door, his eyes never leaving hers. He nodded toward the jewelry cabinets. "You got questions?"

She dropped her gaze to the cases and said nothing.

"You do, you come to me. Got it?"

"Got it." She moved to leave, but he blocked her again. He nodded toward the cabinet.

"How much did he show you?" He could see the mortified expression on her face.

"Enough."

"Enough?" He studied her closely. "Maybe Rory was right."

"About what?"

"Maybe you do need to know just what it is we do here."

She lifted her chin. "I know what you do."

He smirked. "Oh, really. Does that also go for the stuff Rory was just showing you?"

"God, yes. Although, why someone would want to get their...their..." She gestured toward his crotch, apparently searching for a pretty word for it. "Junk pierced is beyond me."

He grinned, knowing this was all making her nervous. "For sexual pleasure, Ava. Can you imagine who'd be getting the most pleasure from that?" When she refused to give him a reply, he answered for her. "The woman."

She made no remark to that, but he didn't miss it when her eyes dropped to his crotch again momentarily. Grinning, he moved toward the multi-drawer cabinet. It was one of those plastic multi-compartment organizers that held three or four dozen little trays or drawers. It was the kind of thing that usually held nuts and bolts, or maybe beads for crafters.

He moved his finger down a row until he came to the tray he was looking for and pulled out the little drawer. He dug out a tiny Ziploc bag and held it up. "Here's something *you* might like."

She frowned, studying the item he held up. They

looked like little silver rings, except one side didn't quite meet.

"What are they?"

"None-piercing nipple rings."

That had her moving back.

"You've never done a rebellious thing in your whole life have you?"

She lifted her chin.

"I dare you."

"Dare me to what?"

"I dare you to try them."

Her eyes got big. "Those?"

"Yes. These."

"What, now?"

He reached out a hand, slipping two fingers in her belt loop of her jeans and tugged her forward a step, then he tucked the little bag in her hip pocket. "Take them home. Wear them tomorrow."

"You're joking, right?"

"Nope." He took in her uneasy face. It wasn't in her wheelhouse; she would never do such a thing. Not without a push, and he was just the man to push. "I'll bet you don't have the guts to do it."

She folded her arms. "Is that so?"

"Yup." He watched her muster her courage, and he

couldn't help the grin that pulled at his mouth. Maybe she had more guts than he gave her credit for. Maybe she'd surprise him.

"Where I come from, you throw out a bet, you have to take one as well."

He pulled his chin up, his eyes narrowing in on her as he contemplated where she was going with this. "What'd you have in mind?"

She bit her lip, contemplating her answer.

He grinned as she appeared to be racking her brain for something she knew he'd fail at. She must have come up with one, because suddenly she was staring him dead in the eye with a smirk on her face.

"I bet you can't go a day without swearing."

Goddamn it, his one weakness. And she knew it, too, the little minx. He'd already shoved so much money in that damn cuss jar he could go broke before the Gala. Well, two can play that game, and it'd be worth every swear word he had to choke down if he could get her to loosen up. *And* tease the hell out of her in the process.

"Deal." He could see by the way she swallowed, the smug expression on her face melting away, that she never expected he'd take her bet. In turn, he'd just forced her hand, meaning she'd have to take his.

***

The next morning, Ava was getting dressed for work. She put the nipple rings on, determined not to lose the stupid bet she never should have taken.

Who cared if he thought her a prude? Maybe she was. What was wrong with that? What difference did it make if he didn't think she had a rebellious bone in her body? Why should she care?

Only she did.

And that was the hell of it.

She wasn't even sure why she cared, she just knew that for some reason she wanted him to have a higher opinion of her than he did. Maybe she wanted to take him down a notch, to prove that he wasn't always right, at least not when it came to her. He thought he had her pegged, and maybe he did, but she'd be damned if she'd let him know that.

Nope, Jameson was not going to win this round.

She finished getting dressed and looked in the mirror. Even with her bra on, the rings made her nipples stand out, protruding proudly like she was in a freezer case, for God's sake. Blast that man. He knew this would happen, and he knew he'd be able to tell if she had them on or not.

Maybe she could wear a sweater, but it was the

middle of summer. She'd look like an idiot. She tried on a dozen different tops, but it didn't matter, they showed through all of them.

Ava bit her lip and glanced toward her dresser. Maybe a padded bra would help, but the only problem was she didn't own one. She'd never needed one. She'd never needed help in that department.

Oh, damn that man! She put a cardigan over her shirt and headed out to work.

By the time she walked into Brothers Ink, it was 11:00 a.m., and the temperature outside was already climbing into the mid-eighties.

They kept the shop cool, but not that cool. Soon she was sweltering. She had no choice but to take it off. Being behind the reception counter, most clients really didn't have a good look at what she wore anyway. Hours passed, and she soon forgot all about it.

At about 7:00 p.m. she got up to get a cup of coffee. The late hours were really starting to take their toll, and most evenings she needed all the caffeine she could get just to make it to the end of the night. She walked into the break room and headed toward the back counter where the coffee maker sat. There was an inch remaining at the bottom of the pot that was probably leftover from earlier in the day. She dumped it in the sink and began filling the glass carafe with water.

Jameson walked in and went to the refrigerator. He cracked open a bottle of water and guzzled down half of it, his eyes on her. She turned to get another box of coffee filters, trying her best to ignore him, but she did glance up as she dumped the old grounds in the trash.

With his chin tilted up as he gulped his water, she saw his eyes drop to her chest. The bottle came down and he gasped for air, his eyes still staring at her blouse. Then she remembered — the damn rings.

Shit.

She quickly turned and finished making the coffee. When she flipped the switch to start the brewing process, she felt him move near her.

***

Jameson couldn't believe what he was seeing. She'd actually done it. She'd actually worn the damn things. He didn't think she had it in her; he'd been so busy today, he'd forgotten about their stupid bet.

Before he realized what he was doing, his hand was on her upper arm, pulling her around. His eyes again focused in on her chest.

She tried to pull free, turning ten shades of red.

He muttered a couple of curse words, and then as if some power was controlling him, he found himself pulling her from the room, down the hall, and into the private room. Slamming the door, he plopped her up on the padded table and moved in close.

"What are you doing?" she snapped, her eyes wide.

"What I shouldn't," he growled. His hands lifted to hold her head still while his mouth came down on hers. It was a kiss meant to communicate that he was not a man to be played with. Maybe this had started as a game between them, and maybe he'd been the one to start it, but he was fast realizing it was a game neither of them had any business playing. So, his kiss was claiming, assertive, meant to say something that no words could. When he finally came up for air, he snapped, "Give up."

It wasn't a request. It came out sounding exactly like he meant it — a demand. He watched the cute little frown lines form between her brows.

"What?" Her voice was barely a whisper.

"This game we're playing, give it up."

"What game?"

"You. Me. Both trying to outlast the other. Give it up. Run back to your safe little office where you belong and get as far away from me as you can."

That little chin of hers came up, like he'd watched it do a dozen times since she'd started working for him, and she insisted, "No. I don't quit. I'm not a quitter."

"This is going to take us down a road neither one of us should go. You know that, don't you?" She nodded, and he watched her eyes drop to his mouth, taking in the tick in his jaw. "And still you're not giving it up?"

"I can't."

"Then don't say I didn't warn you." He stared down at her mouth, then pushed away and left her staring after him. He was sure, like him, she was wondering what the fuck just happened between them. Something had changed. Something big. Something had shifted, and it had shifted in a way they both knew, without a doubt, it would never shift back.

***

That night, Ava lay in bed and thought about that kiss. She couldn't deny that it had aroused her. Jameson was a great kisser, and she liked the way he was so confident and assertive in everything he did. He knew exactly who he was and made no excuses. He was all man, and he definitely knew how to go after a woman. He could have her heart pounding with just one look.

He challenged her. She'd never had a man do that before. Not the way he did. Not the way he got inside her head, knew what she was thinking before she even spoke.

Today he'd pushed her to her limits and maybe beyond, daring her to do something she never would have without that push. She'd surprised more than herself today. She'd surprised him. She'd seen it in his eyes, and it had felt *good*. Knowing she could push him off balance just as he did her.

She also knew it was his plan to push her beyond her limits in order to get her to quit. There was no way in hell that was happening. She couldn't let it.

Biting her lip, her only worry was just how far this game could go before the Gala rolled around.

CHAPTER SIXTEEN

Ava looked up when she heard someone come through the front door of the shop. It had been several days since her and Jameson had their little confrontation. In the subsequent days, they'd both fallen into an uneasy stalemate. Jameson was out of the shop at the moment, and that was fine with Ava. It seemed it was the only time she could truly relax, because anytime he was in the building her whole body tingled with awareness of him.

Ava watched a woman enter. She appeared to be young, possibly even college age. She was rail thin, had long dark hair, and heavy eye makeup. She walked up to the counter.

"Is Jameson here?"

Ava smiled up at the girl. "He's not at the moment. May I help you? Did you want to make an appointment?"

The young woman eyed her coldly. "I don't remember you from last time."

"I haven't been here long," Ava informed her,

watching the girl's eyes run up and down her.

The girl cocked her head. "You're his latest plaything, aren't you?"

Ava gave her an arch look. "I beg your pardon?"

The girl shrugged. "It's not your fault. I understand."

"Understand what?" Ava snapped with a bite to her words.

"You're his latest toy. His meantime girl."

"*Meantime girl?*"

"Yes, until I finish school and come back home. You wouldn't be the first."

Liam walked up, folding his thick arms. "Rachel. What are you doing here?"

Ava eyed him, noting the unwelcoming stance and cold look in his eyes.

"I came to see Jamie, of course."

"Get out, Rachel. Jameson is through with you. He told you that. Repeatedly."

"That's between me and Jameson now, isn't it? You need to mind your own business."

Liam's arms came unfolded, and Ava watched as the laidback man she knew became a true brother about to stick up for his sibling.

"This *is* my business. You're standin' in it. So, I

suggest it's *you* that needs to move along and mind your business."

"Jamie won't like the way you're talking to me."

"Jamie won't give a damn."

"I'm not leaving until I talk to him."

"He's not even here, bitch."

"Why don't you call him?" Ava suggested to the girl, whose eyes cut to her.

Liam jumped at that comment before the girl could reply. "Because he's blocked her calls. Isn't that right, Rachel?"

"You just need to shut up, Liam. This doesn't involve you."

"And you need to get the fuck out. Now." He took a threatening step toward her. She immediately backed against the door.

"I'll be back!"

"Then I'll have the pleasure of watching Jameson throw your ass out. That's a show I'd pay to see."

"To hell with you," she snapped as she stormed out. They watched her stalk past the plate glass window flipping them off as she went.

Ava looked at Liam, her mouth open. "Oh, my God. What was that about?"

"Just a delusional stalker bitch from Jameson's

past. Don't let her get to you."

"Were they a couple?"

"Fuck no! She's messed up in the head. He did some ink for her, was kind to her, and she built it up in her head that it was more than it was. Suddenly, she's convinced she's his girl." Liam paused to shake his head. "Couldn't be further from the truth."

Ava looked toward the window. "Will she be back?"

Liam ruffled her head. "Don't worry, darlin'. She comes back, I'll run her ass off again. As a matter of fact, I think I'll call and let Jamie know." He pulled out his phone, his thumb moving over the screen, and then put it on speaker.

Ava watched, riveted as Jameson picked up.

"Yeah?"

Liam grinned, his eyes connecting with Ava's as he spoke. "Hey, man. Your *special little friend* came by to pay you a visit."

"Are you fucking serious?"

"Yup. And you're on speaker, so the cuss jar meter is running."

"Take me off fucking speaker, asshole."

Liam chuckled, his eyes sparkling at Ava as he put the phone to his ear. "Yeah, you're off."

Ava turned away, not sure what to make of all that. She'd known Jameson had some near-groupie-level fans, but stalkers? That was a bit much. She definitely had felt the woman's anger directed at her when the girl had found her in the shop. She certainly didn't want to walk out to her car one night and find her tires slashed or her car keyed. She wondered just how crazy this girl was.

Liam finished the call with Jameson and slid his phone into his pocket, his eyes on her. "Don't worry about it. Jamie will handle her."

"Bet that call put him in a great mood," she remarked, rolling her eyes.

"Actually, he was more concerned about you," Liam replied, dipping his head to look at her.

"Me? Why?"

"He knows how toxic that girl can be and the garbage that can spew out of her mouth. He was worried she had upset you." Liam's brows shot up as if that was a revelation.

Ava frowned. Jamie concerned about her? The man actually had feelings and concern for others? Amazing… and confusing. He hated her, didn't he? Why would he be concerned about her? Hmm. Maybe he didn't really hate her. Maybe it was all an act just to get her to quit. He hadn't seemed to hate her yesterday when he'd dragged her into the private room.

Liam returned to his station, and Ava tried to put it out of her head as she got back to work.

Ten minutes later, she heard the door open and turned to look. It was the same girl again. Ava barely had time to note the super-sized soft drink cup in her hand before the girl was across the space and tossing the drink in her face.

Ava could only suck in a stunned breath as the cold liquid and ice completely covered her front, soaking through her blouse and skirt.

The girl violently threw the cup on the ground and ran out the door, even as Liam and Max both bolted from their stations. Liam charged to the door, throwing it open and stepping out onto the sidewalk. He glanced both directions, but the girl was long gone.

Max squatted down next to Ava's chair. "Babe, you okay?"

"*Oh, my God!* Why would she do that?" She looked down at her ruined outfit. "I'm soaked."

Max tried to help her up as Liam approached.

"There are some towels in the back. Come on, let's get you cleaned up," Max offered in a calm voice.

Ava noticed Liam pull his phone out and put it to

his ear. As Max led her to the back, she heard Liam snap, "Get over here, now."

Ava went into the bathroom with the towels Max brought her and did the best she could to dry off. There was a tap at the door. Max's voice came through the solid wood.

"I've got a shop t-shirt from the display case that you can put on, Ava."

She opened the door a few inches and took the item he held out. Smiling, she thanked him. After closing the door, she removed her silk blouse. The caramel-colored soda had stained it horribly. She tossed it in the garbage can and dried off her skin. She did the best she could to absorb the wetness that had seeped into her bra, which she wasn't about to remove. Slipping the t-shirt on, she ran the towel over her skirt. There was a big wet spot, but she'd have to wear it home. She dried her face again, looking at herself in the mirror above the sink. At least, the girl hadn't gotten too much of it in her hair.

As she studied her reflection, she began to wonder if she'd bitten off more than she could chew with this crazy deal. She angrily tossed the wet towel in the corner. Jameson obviously didn't want her there, and if this was the abuse she was going to have to put up with on a regular basis, she seriously considered throwing in the towel.

She opened the door and stepped out.

Liam was leaning against the wall, his arms folded, his head down. He looked up when she emerged.

"You okay?"

She nodded. "I'm sure I look like hell, but I'm fine."

"Jamie's on his way."

She wasn't sure what that was supposed to mean, but she nodded. Then she headed toward her desk.

"I'll drive you home if you want. I'm sure Jamie would understand if you took the rest of the day off."

"We have a deal. I'm not giving him an excuse to say I didn't fulfill my end of it." She reached her desk with Liam following behind her. He came around and stood at the counter as she dug through her purse for a hairbrush.

"Ava, Jamie is not going to think you're welching for going home after what just happened."

She violently tugged the brush through her hair, her shock beginning to be replaced by anger. "I'm fine, okay? Just leave it alone, Liam."

He didn't look happy, but he nodded and walked off. She was sorry she'd snapped at him, but her nerves were a little frazzled. Perhaps she should focus her anger on Jameson, she thought to herself... and imagined throwing a drink at *him*.

***

A half hour later, the man himself strode in the front door. He walked straight to her, coming around the counter. Surprised, she swiveled her chair to stare up at him.

"You okay?"

She noted the genuine concern in his eyes and admitted quietly, "I'm fine."

He studied her, as if weighing the truth of her words. "She won't bother you again. I promise you."

"All right."

"Come on."

She frowned up at him. He said nothing, just reached past her to grab her purse, and then took her hand, pulling her from her chair. She followed behind him; it wasn't like she had any choice in the matter. "Where are we going?"

He led her toward the door. "I'm taking you home."

She pulled back. "Jameson, I'm fine."

He stopped, his eyes telling her not to argue. They stared at each other long enough for the silent communication between them. She closed her mouth, and he continued to the door, her hand still clenched in his.

He led her to a pickup truck parked two spots from the door. It was a big shiny black crew cab.

Jameson moved to the passenger side and opened the door for her. The lift-kit had her hiking her skirt to climb in. When he made sure she was seated, he closed the door and walked to the driver's side.

Ava looked around at the spotless cab of the truck, noting the new-car smell that still permeated the interior. The driver door opened, and the truck rocked as he climbed in.

He glanced over at her. "Buckle up."

In a haze, she did as she was told. When her belt was clicked into place, he started the truck up and backed out of the diagonal spot. He spun the steering wheel with his palm as he maneuvered the big vehicle.

"What's your address?"

She gave it to him.

He returned his eyes to the road, and Ava noted a quiet rock station played in the background as they rode silently through town.

He pulled to the curb in front of her house. "This it?"

"Yes, thank you." She reached for the door handle,

but his words stopped her.

"Look, Ava, I'm sorry about what happened. That had nothing to do with you; you just got caught in the crossfire and you never should have."

"I can take it. I'm tougher than you think."

"I'm finding that out."

She glanced down at herself, wondering at the turn the conversation seemed to have taken and tried to lighten the mood. "At least I got a free shirt out of it."

The corner of his mouth lifted slightly. "Silver-lining kind of girl, huh?"

She looked down, plucking at the hem. "I try to be."

"I'll pay for the blouse."

She met his eyes. "That's not necessary."

"Yeah, it is."

"Okay, then. I'll let you."

He surprised her by grasping her chin in his hand and pulling her closer, staring intently into her eyes. "What I said yesterday in the supply room? I meant it."

She knew right away what he was talking about. When he'd told her to quit. She tried to pull her chin up, but he held it. "I did, too."

He studied her a long moment, his eyes dropping to her mouth, and for a second she thought he was going to kiss her again. But then he seemed to pull himself back, murmuring, "See you tomorrow."

She was surprised by the letdown that swelled inside her when he didn't kiss her, but she didn't acknowledge it. Instead she frowned. "I can just go in and change if you want to wait."

He shook his head. "Take the rest of the night off."

"You're sure?"

"Yeah. Least I can do after tonight."

She swung her door open. "All right, then. Goodnight."

"Goodnight."

She climbed out and turned to watch him leave, but he sat parked, waiting for her to get inside. She moved up the walk, up the two steps onto her craftsman style porch, and fumbled with her keys in the lock. It wasn't until she had the door open that she heard the big truck's engine as it pulled away.

CHAPTER SEVENTEEN

Late the next night, around 8:00, Ava realized the last customer had left. She pulled up the calendar in the computer and frowned at the entry she hadn't noticed before.

Landry Party, it read.

Every artist's time was blocked off. She thought that was odd.

Max, Liam, and Rory wandered up to the lobby.

Max folded his arms and leaned back against her counter, his eyes on Rory. "How well do you know this girl?"

Rory stood with his hands in his pockets, his feet spread wide. "She's our drummer's fiancée."

Liam moved to sit on the sofa, his arms stretching along the back. "She cute?"

Rory grinned over at Liam. "She's a knockout. Her whole posse is. Don't worry, Bro. You won't mind working on any of them."

"They're all getting a piercing?" Max asked.

Rory shrugged. "Don't know. Think some are just

coming along for the fun. There'll probably be a few partying."

Ava frowned. "What's going on, guys?"

Max looked over his shoulder at her. "Didn't anybody tell you? Bachelorette party is coming in tonight. Rory shoulda told you. It's his deal."

Her eyes cut to Rory. "A bachelorette party? Why would they come here for God's sake?"

Rory grinned big. "They're all getting their bellybuttons pierced."

"A bellybutton piercing party?" she joked with arched brows.

"Suppose you could call it that."

Liam teased, "Isn't that what all you women do on a Saturday night?"

"Where I come from we have Tupperware parties."

Jameson walked up, giving her a grin. "This'll be a whole lot more fun than a Tupperware party, sweetheart. You gonna be able to let go of all those repressive attitudes and have some fun?"

"Fun? What fun will I be having? I'm working the desk."

Jameson grinned, then cut his eyes to Rory. "We need some music."

Rory grinned back and moved to the sound system.

"Absolutely."

A moment later, a driving rock beat filled the shop and about twenty girls came through the door. Although they all had cheap tiaras on their heads and feathered boas around their necks, the bride-to-be was easy to spot. She was dressed in white short-shorts, a tight white tank with bride spelled out across her chest in rhinestones, and a veil attached to the back of her tiara.

"Welcome, ladies," Rory greeted them, and then kissed the bride. "Stacy, love, you look beautiful. Sure I can't steal you away from Gary?"

She kissed his cheek. "I won't stop you from trying, hon."

"So ladies, are you all getting piercings tonight?" Rory asked.

There was some loud whooping.

"If you are, we need releases signed. Ava, here, will help you with that. We'll be locking the door and flipping the closed sign for your party. I see some of you brought some refreshments—"

Another high-pitched whoop went up as drink cups were raised in the air.

Rory continued, "We just ask that if any of you want a tattoo, that you aren't drinking. If you are, we can schedule you to come back for that."

"What about piercings?" one of them shouted from the back. "Can we get one of those?"

Rory chuckled. "Piercings should be fine."

A girl in the back pushed through the crowd with a stack of plastic shot glasses and a bottle in her hand. "Good, because I brought the Fireball!"

Another whoop went up in the air.

"We've got a display case full of jewelry for you to look through. If you don't see what you're looking for, hit me up and I might have something in the back I can show you."

"I'll just bet you do, Rory!" one of the girls called out. The others all hooted and Rory grinned big, waggling his brows.

Liam took a stack of release forms from Ava and began passing them around. "Fill these out, and we'll need to see IDs, ladies."

And so the party commenced. Ava couldn't believe this was happening. Girls who soon had the forms filled out were either shopping the jewelry case or dancing to the music and doing shots. If she didn't know better, she would think she was in a nightclub.

Jameson leaned on the counter. "How about you, babe? You up for getting a piercing tonight?"

"I'm working," she hedged.

Jameson turned to one of the women, but his eyes stayed on Ava when he said, "I like when a woman is brave enough to let loose, go wild, face her fears…"

The girl held her glass in the air, whooped, and bumped hips with him.

He smiled, his brows arching. "Well?"

Ava lifted her chin, determined to show him. "Fine. Let's go."

He grinned as she stood, shoving her chair back. He swept his arm out, indicating the jewelry case across the lobby. "On the house, sweetheart. Anything you want."

She glared at him, but held her head high as she moved around the counter and headed toward the case. She bent and peered at all the different styles. Her eyes were drawn to the sparkling crystal designs. There were flowers, hearts, dolphins, butterflies, angel wings, even spiders. She settled on a simple round pink crystal attached to a curved barbell and pointed to it. "That one."

Jameson glanced at it, nodded, and then grabbed a release form. After she'd signed it, he said, "Follow me."

He led her through the crowd of girls who were

getting piercings in the main area and back to the private piercing room. Stepping inside, he helped her up on the table.

"Lie back."

When she did, he moved off to dig through the cabinet for the ring she'd picked out, searching by its stock number. She glanced around nervously. She'd been in this room before, but it was completely different when she was the one on the table. There was a full-length mirror on one wall, and she rolled her head to look. She could see her reflection staring back at her, and the look in her eyes said, *what the hell are you doing up on that table, girl?*

Jameson pulled over a rolling tray and set up with the needed supplies. She glanced over and saw a pair of clamps, a couple of swab sticks, her jewelry, and a white packet marked *14 Gauge Curved Needle, Sterile*.

"You an innie or an outie?"

She frowned. "Beg your pardon?"

"Not everyone is a good candidate for a navel piercing. Outies get in the way, so innies work best."

"I'm an innie."

"Let's see." He lifted his chin, motioning for her to pull her shirt up.

When her belly was exposed, his eyes moved over it, and not just in a professional way either. She caught a flash of something in his expression that told her he was more affected by the sight of her smooth skin than he should be.

"Good," he murmured.

The piercing room was immaculately clean, and the padded table had a protective paper cover that crackled when she shifted. A quick look around the room revealed bottles of disinfectant nearby and a hand sink.

Jameson moved to it and began washing his hands thoroughly.

"Um, is it going to hurt?" she asked in a quiet voice.

He glanced toward her. "Everyone has their own personal pain threshold, but don't worry, sweetheart, this type of piercing is not as painful as it looks." He winked at her. "I'll let you in on a little secret. Women take pain better than men."

She smiled, grateful for his assurance even if she wasn't sure it was true.

He pulled some paper towels and dried his hands, and then reached in a small paper box, grabbed out a disposable oval shaped mask, and hung it around his neck. Then he reached in another box and pulled out a pair of black latex gloves. He turned to her as he snapped them on.

"You don't have any latex allergies, do you?"

Ava shook her head.

He cocked his head to the side. "You nervous?"

She frowned. "Why do you have a mask?"

"All this good hygiene goes toward lowering the possibility of transmitting blood borne diseases such as HIV and hepatitis. Not saying you have those; it's just safe practice all shops should follow for blood borne pathogens."

He moved toward her, reaching up to push her shirt further out of the way. He must have noticed the way her stomach trembled.

"You didn't answer my question earlier. You nervous?"

"A little."

He reached up on a shelf and retrieved something. Then he held it out to her. "Stress ball. Sometimes they help."

She smiled and took it. "Thanks."

"This will be a little cold." He scrubbed her navel with a surgical wash to sterilize the area. His eyes flicked up to hers as she jumped at the coolness. "I usually don't have the need to apply topical anesthetic for this, but I do keep it on hand for the especially squeamish."

"I'm fine."

"You'll feel some pain, but most people describe it as a momentary pinch or prick."

"Okay."

"First I have to mark you. It's best to stand up." He held his hand out and helped her off the table. Then he positioned her in front of the stool he sat on and picked up a surgical marking pen. He made a mark about a centimeter above her belly button and then one inside.

Ava found it awkward having his head bent so close to her exposed belly. She watched as he picked up the jewelry she'd chosen off the tray and unscrewed the top. Then he held the barbell up to the marks, checking the length. When he was satisfied, he pulled back and gestured toward the mirror. "Check and see if you're happy with where I marked it."

She moved to look.

"Is it aligned horizontally?" he asked.

"It looks like it."

"Okay then?"

She nodded.

He patted the table and grinned. "Now comes the fun part."

She climbed up and reclined back.

He put his mask up and tore open the needle

packet. The crinkling noise seemed especially loud in the quiet room as she lay there nervously anticipating the needle puncturing her skin. When she saw the thickness of the needle, she took a breath and blew it out through her mouth slowly.

He glanced over. "You okay?"

She nodded, watching as he slid a rubber band around the handle of the clamps. "I just didn't realize the needle would be so big."

"It'll be quick. You feel light-headed? Nauseous?"

She shook her head.

"Talk to me so I know you're good."

"I'm fine. It's just the waiting."

He turned toward her and tapped her nearest arm. "Move this arm, sweetheart."

She did.

"That's good. Right there."

She watched his hands as he lined up the clamps with the marks he'd made.

"This will pinch," he warned. "Take a deep breath and let it out slowly. I'm gonna pierce on the exhale."

Aligning the sharp end of the needle with the mark on the underside of the clamp, he pierced from the bottom up with one fluid movement pushing the needle through the skin, making sure it exited through the mark at the top of the clamp. He quickly slid the barbell into the needle and pushed it through.

"And you're done."

He took the loose ball and screwed it tightly onto the top of the barbell. Then he took a swab stick with solution and very gently — and thoroughly — cleaned around the piercing. It stung, and he glanced up when she flinched.

"Does that burn?"

"Just a bit."

"Was it as bad as you thought?"

She shook her head. "No. I've had a bee sting hurt worse than that."

"See, not so bad. Like I told you, just a pinch. The clamp probably hurts more than needle, right?"

She smiled. "Right." Lifting her head, she glanced down at it. "How do I clean it?"

"I'll give you a spray. It's antibacterial."

"Oh, okay."

He pulled his gloves off with a snap and held his hand out to help steady her as she jumped down. He gestured toward the mirror. "Have a look."

She held her shirt up and moved to the glass. She caught his reflection as he sat on the stool, pulling his mask down. He watched her, smiling.

"Happy?"

She dropped one hand toward it, wanting to touch it. It seemed so foreign.

"Don't touch it."

She paused and looked at him.

"It's natural to feel preoccupied with your new goodie, but playing with it will only lead to infection."

"Okay."

"A new piercing is like an open wound, so it is extremely important that you maintain a strict cleaning regime over the next couple of months. You'll need to keep it up until the piercing heals completely in order to prevent any itching or infection."

"All right."

He moved to a shelf and took a sheet of paper off a stack. Then he grabbed the spray he'd said he'd give her. "Follow these directions and always wash your hands before touching your piercing. Avoid fiddling with it."

"Okay."

"And no swimming or baths until you are completely healed."

"When will that be?"

"Most likely three or four months, but occasionally they can take as long as twelve months. Once the outer area is healed the inside of the piercing still takes a while to toughen up until you no longer feel any twinges of pain."

"I see."

"Hopefully you're happy with it and will be proud to show it off."

"Show it off?"

"Yeah. Girls don't get those piercings to cover them up."

"I...I'm not sure why I did it. I'm really not the type to wear tops that show my bellybutton."

"So what was the point in getting it?"

She turned away.

"Hey?"

She wouldn't turn around, but she moved her head slightly to the side to let him know she was listening.

"I pushed you into it, didn't I?" He shook his head almost as if he was disappointed in her. "You didn't even want it, did you? And here I thought maybe you had a bit of wild in you after all. Guess I was wrong."

She looked away, but wouldn't admit it. "I need to get back out there." She moved to the door, opened it, and walked out.

***

Jameson let her go, wondering why pushing her

hadn't ended up feeling as good as he thought it would.

***

Ava returned to her desk. The party was still going on, girls waiting their turn to get pierced, but she was oblivious to it all. Jameson's words echoed through her head. *I pushed you into it, didn't I?*

He didn't think she could be wild without being pushed—like she was a geeky little schoolgirl who'd never done a wild thing in her life. Her chin came up. She'd show him. Not here, not now. But tomorrow she'd show the *King of Ink* just how wild she could be.

CHAPTER EIGHTEEN

The next evening, after the shop had closed, Ava sat on the padded table in the private tattooing room. Liam was on a stool pulled up to her.

"The design we come up with depends on where you want to put it. Have you decided?"

"Um. Well…"

At her hesitation, he qualified in a quiet voice, "It tells me how much space I have to work with."

She bit her lip. She knew he was trying to put her at ease, and it wasn't that the spot was all that intimate, but still, she'd have to pull her shirt up. Suddenly being alone in the room with Liam, even though she felt safe with him, just felt a little *too* intimate. After all, she worked with the man.

"Sweetheart, I do this for a living, and I've seen it all, but if you're changing your mind or want to think about it—"

"No, I want it done," she replied sharply. "Today. It has to be today."

That had him frowning. "There a reason for the

rush all of a sudden?"

There was, but she'd be damned if she'd admit the reason was because Jameson had goaded her, and because of it, she now felt she had something to prove.

"Ava, if you get a tattoo, it should be because you really want it. And you've thought about it for a long time."

"I do. I have. Thought about it, I mean. I've been thinking about it since the moment I walked in the shop. Maybe even before that. I think it's been in the back of my mind for a long time."

"All right. What did you want?"

"If I tell you something, do you promise not to say anything to Jameson?"

He searched her eyes. "If that's what you want."

"The tattoo, it's for my sister. She passed away a few years ago."

He pulled back slightly at the news. "I'm sorry, Ava. I had no idea."

She nodded, looking down and plucking at the hem of her shirt. "Thank you."

"A memorial, then? Did you know what you wanted?"

"I...I drew this." She pulled a scrap of paper out of her pocket. It was a pencil sketch she'd done of some flowers.

He took it, his eyes moving over it.

"I'm not very artistic." She shrugged. "Maybe just her name would be better," she finished lamely, thinking her drawing suddenly looked like the work of a five-year-old.

He gave her a smile. "They're real pretty. Why don't you tell me about your sister and maybe together we can come up with something."

Ava sucked her lips in. It was hard even now to talk about her. Liam's eyes searched hers, and she knew he could see how hard it was.

"Okay, honey. How about we start with where you want to put it?"

She gave him a thankful smile and leaned to the side, pulling her shirt up to reveal her ribs. The door opened suddenly and they both glanced up, startled. Liam twisted toward the door behind him, and Ava peered over his head to see Jameson standing there looking pissed as hell.

His eyes drilled into hers, ignoring his brother. "Absolutely not."

She frowned at his odd comment, dropping her shirt as Liam stood and turned to face his brother. "You know better than to barge in here like this, Jamie."

Jameson's eyes cut to him. "Give us a minute."

Liam glanced back over his shoulder at Ava, as if to ask if she was okay with that. Her eyes met his, and she nodded. With that, Liam moved to leave, but not before giving his brother a stern look as he left.

Jameson watched out of the corner of his eye as Liam closed the door behind him. Then his gaze fell on her.

She sat on the padded table waiting, not sure what would come out of his mouth. But what she heard was the last thing she expected.

"I think maybe I pushed you too far." His words were softly spoken, almost as if admitting something that pained him.

She frowned. Was he talking about the bellybutton ring from last night? Did he think that was what she and Liam were in here doing? Checking her piercing? She shook her head. "The piercing is beautiful. I don't regret it."

He shook his head. "Not talking about the piercing. Although, I'm happy to hear you're pleased." He held her gaze. "I know why you're in here. You were going to let him tattoo you, weren't you?"

She looked away, her jaw clenching. *Damn it.* She'd wanted it over and done with before he found out. She supposed Max must have told him. It would explain why he'd seemed pissed off before he'd even opened the door.

"Weren't you?" he pressed.

Her eyes snapped back to his. "It's not your business. That's between me and my tattoo artist."

"Your tattoo artist? Right." He held her eyes, and there was a wealth of communication there, only she was incapable of deciphering it. She broke his gaze, wondering just how well he could read *her* and not wanting to give away how his very presence affected her. That didn't stop him from continuing as he came closer, "Anybody tattoos you, Ava, it'll be me."

She turned wide eyes on him. "You?"

"But not before we have a talk, an honest conversation."

"What do we have to talk about? How much you hate me? How nothing I do is good enough for you?"

He folded his arms, and her eyes couldn't help but run over the tattooed muscles, distracting her from her anger until his words brought her eyes up.

"I don't hate you, Ava." He looked away and blew out a frustrated breath. "Look, last night I egged you on. I was trying to push you past your limits, and part of that, I'll admit, was that I didn't think you belonged here from the start. Maybe I was trying to prove that to you. Hell, I've been trying to get under your skin since you walked in the door. But pushing a person into a body modification when it's not what they want? That goes against everything I stand for, every principal I built this shop around."

Her chin came up. She wasn't about to let him off the hook that easy. Not when it sounded like he was on the verge of admitting he was wrong and, God forbid, actually apologize for it.

He shifted on his feet, rocking back on his heels. "It was wrong, what I did to you last night. I felt like shit about it afterward. What I'm trying to say is, I'm sorry."

She nodded, and yes, part of her wanted to throw his apology back in his face, to treat his apology the way he had hers just out of spite. But the contention between them had to stop somewhere, and she knew she had to be the one to reach out and take the olive branch he was unexpectedly extending. "Okay. Accepted."

"So you don't have to go through with this. If your purpose was to make a point to me—"

She cut him off. "Maybe I want the tattoo. Ever think of that?"

He cocked his head. "You really want a tattoo? *You?*"

"What's that supposed to mean? I'm not the right 'type' to get a tattoo? Now who's being narrow-minded, Mr. Rebellious?"

"I didn't mean it that way." He held his hand palm up in supplication. "It's just I never figured you'd—"

"I'd what? Have the guts?"

"Don't put words in my mouth, Ava."

She huffed out a breath, folding her arms. "Fine. Then explain."

"Look, I just don't want you to have any regrets. But if you want this, *really* want this, I'm all for it. I believe in self-expression. All forms." He paused, searching her eyes. "So, do you?"

She looked away, considering. Now that it wouldn't have the desired punch she'd first intended, *did* she still want it? She thought about the time she'd spent last night carefully drawing out her idea as best she could and all the emotions that she'd felt and the love she'd tried to put into the design. So, in answer to his question, yes, she did. She suddenly found herself wanting it more than anything.

Her eyes met his. "Yes. I do."

"It's not to prove something to me? Because, babe,

you've got nothing to prove to me. Not one damn thing."

She shook her head. "It's for me."

"Okay..." He drew the word out, almost like he wasn't sure he believed her. His eyes studied hers closely and he frowned. "What did you want?"

"Liam was going to do it." She wasn't sure she could bear to tell him about her sister. That would mean opening up to him. Really opening up.

Again he studied her a long moment before stating quietly, "I'd like to do it, if you'll let me."

"I don't know..." She looked away.

He moved to sit on the stool in front of her and put his palms on either side of her knees, looking up at her. "We've got to start learning to trust each other sometime, Ava. Me with your ideas about the shop, and maybe you with this."

She stared at him, her mouth dropping open. "You're going with my ideas?"

A small smile tugged at the corner of his mouth. "I'm considering them, let's just put it that way. Good enough?"

The smile she gave him in return was blinding. "Good enough."

He lifted his chin. "So tell me what you decided on.

What was Liam going to ink on that pretty body of yours?"

She heard his offhanded compliment, and a strange feeling shot through her. "Well, we hadn't worked that out yet."

He noticed the scrap of paper on the padded table next to her hip and picked it up. "You draw this?"

She nodded. "It was just an idea I had. It doesn't have to be exactly that."

He looked up at her. "Where did you want to put it?"

"My ribs, by my heart."

"Oow. Babe, that can be a really painful area."

"Oh, I hadn't thought of that."

"How big we talkin'?"

She shrugged.

He lifted his chin. "Lie back a second."

She did as he bid, eyeing him curiously.

"Turn on your side."

When she did, he tugged the hem of her shirt up just a bit and indicated with his hand the area from her waist down along the top of her hip. "How about something a little lower? Get it off your ribs. This area can be really beautiful curving down along your side."

She studied the area he suggested.

"Looks sexy as hell with a bikini," he teased with a wink.

This softer, teasing side of him was throwing her for a loop. Suddenly he was behaving with her like she'd seen him behave with other female customers, turning on the charm and the full potency of his charisma. She found she couldn't help but smile back at him.

"All right."

He looked again at her drawing. "Mind if I sketch something out for you. Something a little more…detailed?"

She nodded. "I want the flower in the middle to be a Lily. The rest, I don't care, but the central flower… It has to be a Lily."

He stared into her eyes a moment. "Is there some significance?"

And suddenly she couldn't tell him, so she looked away. "I just… think they're pretty."

He nodded. "Okay then. That's what you want, that's what you'll get. Can you give me a few minutes to sketch something out?"

"Of course."

He offered his hand as she hopped down off the table. "Half hour?"

She nodded, and they both left the room. She headed to the front, and he headed up to his office. It was after hours, which was why Liam had time to do it for her, but all three brothers sat watching as she emerged with Jameson.

"What happened? You still want the tattoo?" Liam asked.

"Yes."

"Then lets get started."

"Liam… Jameson wants to do it."

That brought his chin up. "He does, does he?"

"Yes." She studied his expression as his eyes moved to the staircase and then back to her.

"I see."

Did he? Because she wasn't sure she did. What had brought about this change in him? Was it the party last night? Pushing her like that? Or was it something more?

Max rolled her chair over from the receptionist area. "Here, love. Sit with us."

She did, and he sat on his rolling stool. Picking up a bottle of beer from his a six-pack on the floor he said, "I'd offer you one, but if you're getting ink tonight, you shouldn't drink."

"That's right. Good thing you drink so much water

all the time. Being good and hydrated really helps," Liam acknowledged.

She began to fidget. Now that she was committed to getting the tattoo, suddenly the anticipation was starting to get to her.

Rory must have noticed. He glanced over from the chair he sat on, the back swiveled around so that he straddled it. He held up his phone, his thumb scrolling over the screen. "Want to hear our new song, Ava?"

She gave him a grateful smile, happy to have her mind distracted. "Yes. Please."

He turned the volume up and held it out for them to hear.

The men spent the next half hour listening to Rory's songs, chatting and doing what they could to make Ava laugh until Jameson came down the stairs. He walked straight over to her, ignoring them all and held out a sketch for her perusal. "What do you think?"

Her eyes dropped from the serious expression on his face to the paper he held in front of her. It was a colorful design with a single lily prominent in the center of the motif, some bougainvillea on either side, surrounded by scrolling and twining vines in an intricate design that trailed upward and downward. It was lovely, and she could imagine it trailing down over the curve of her hip.

"It's beautiful."

"What you had in mind?"

"It's better."

Jameson nodded once, apparently relieved that she was pleased. "And the colors?"

Her gaze again fell to the drawing. Bright pinks and oranges entwined with vivid shades of green. "They're gorgeous."

"Good. Let's get started."

"Now?"

"No time like the present." He cocked his head. "Unless you've changed your mind?"

Her chin came up. "No. Now is good."

He smiled, stepped back, and extended his hand for her to precede him into the private room.

**

Two hours later, Ava was on the table, the design had been transferred and Jameson was leaning over her hip, applying needle to skin. She was mostly on her back with her hip canted slightly. Lifting her head, she watched as his black-gloved hands worked, one holding the machine, one wiping at the excess ink. She put her head back down and took a deep breath, blowing it out through her mouth.

His eyes flicked up to her. "You doing okay, sweetheart?"

She nodded, staring at the ceiling. "I'm okay."

"If you need to tap out, we can take a break."

"No, I'm good."

He started back up and buzzing filled the room again.

"What do you like about tattooing?" she asked to get her mind off of the shader needles piercing her skin as he worked to add color to the design he'd created.

"This industry, for the most part, is a community of fun and creative people. I was drawn to that. These days, tattoos are accepted as an art form and an outlet of self-expression. Not just for rock stars, bikers, and people of questionable character, but for everyone. It's a centuries-old art. I dig that. For me it's more than just laying ink on someone's skin. It's long been regarded as taboo, but now, finally there's this whole evolution going on that's raising its status as an art form. It's no longer just for the rebel crowd or the unconventional. You'll see doctors and lawyers with ink. We get people from all walks of life coming into the shop now. I think that's cool as hell."

"I suppose that's true."

The buzzing continued to fill the void of

conversation. To get her mind off it, she asked another question. "So, Jameson, did you always want to do this?"

He glanced at her with a grin. "What, tattoo you?"

She chuckled. "Become a tattoo artist."

He turned his attention back to her hip, swiping it with the cloth before starting another area. "Actually, I wanted to be a therapist or counselor of some kind."

"Max told me your parents were killed in a car accident when you both were teenagers.

His gaze shot to her. "He did, huh?"

She nodded. "I'm sorry."

"Thanks. When the accident happened, all those plans of mine went out the window." He shrugged. "I always liked art. This way I get to be creative, and I still get to hear people tell me their stories. You wouldn't believe the things people tell their tattoo artist. I guess it's an intimate thing. You're bent over them, touching their skin, close." His eyes shot to hers, and a smile pulled at his mouth. "Kind of like I am now."

She chuckled. "Right."

He swiped at her skin again, changing position.

"You could have been a bartender," she teased with a smile.

He shook his head. "Naw. The drunks would have

gotten on my nerves, and I would have ended up busting heads. Where're the tips in that?"

"I'm sure the ladies would have loved you. *And tipped you well.*"

He grinned, his eyes shifting to hers for a split second. "The ladies still do love me. Now they just pay me several hundred bucks if they want my undivided attention."

"I see."

"And this way I don't have to mop up spilled beer and puke."

"Gotcha." She paused, studying him. "You have a nice manner when you tattoo."

His eyes flicked up to hers. "Why thanks, sweetheart."

She shifted her arms. Folding them and grasping her wrists, she rested them against her forehead. She stared at the ceiling, blowing a slow breath out, and then her eyes dropped to him, his head bent over her as he worked. "I've watched you with clients, especially women. You're always so gentle with them."

"No reason I shouldn't be. Besides, it keeps 'em coming back for more." He winked.

"I like this side of you, Jameson. You can be quite charming when you want to be."

"I'm big on the upsell. I can always talk a woman into coming back for more. If not a tattoo, at least a piercing or two." He waggled his brows, downplaying her compliment.

"Hmm. I've noticed."

"Have you, now?"

***

Jameson was more moved by her compliment than he'd pretended to be. And that wasn't the only thing that had affected him about this particular session. As he'd cleaned and prepped Ava's hip, the whole while feeling her eyes on his every move, he couldn't deny it felt different, more intimate than it ever had before. Then when he'd placed the stencil, his fingers running over her soft skin, the warmth of her body, her intoxicating smell so close it had him breathing heavier than normal, he definitely knew this was unlike any other time he'd worked on a woman, no matter how beautiful she was.

Ink on skin—it was his art, and as such deserved his best effort, especially a canvas like this one.

Ava's skin was such a contrast under his hands; soft, untouched pale skin to his own big hands and muscled arms covered in ink. *Beauty and the Beast* came to mind; she had about as much business being here, that was a fact. No matter what she'd said, he still felt some guilt that he'd pushed her to this, pushed her too far in this game to bring out her rebellious side. If she ever came to regret this tattoo, he knew he'd never forgive himself. All that aside, having her on his table was arousing beyond belief.

Usually Jameson was all business when working on a client—men, women, didn't matter. But having his hands on Ava affected him like none ever had. Feeling her warm skin under his fingertips, even with the gloves on, he could feel it; the heat radiated off her. Her femininity couldn't be missed. There was something so erotic about his hands marking her skin—marking her with his art. It felt primal, like he was marking her as his in some way. It was a feeling he'd never before had.

Knowing she watched his every move made it that much hotter. Knowing she was entrusting him with her body, especially after the animosity between them, spoke volumes, and he didn't take that lightly.

Trying to keep his professionalism intact, he tried to drive the endless parade of dirty thoughts from his mind.

***

Another hour later, Jameson finally turned off his machine, set it aside, and wiped the design clean. He held a hand mirror out to Ava. "What do you think?"

She took it and looked. Although the design was only about eight inches in length, it was stunning. The vibrant colors climbed along the curve of her hip.

"It's beautiful." Her eyes were suddenly glassy with tears as she thought of her sister.

Jameson grabbed a box of tissues, offering them to her. "Here, babe."

She snatched one out. "I'm sorry. I wasn't expecting to react like this."

He grinned. "I usually don't get that kind of reaction from flowers."

She dabbed at her eyes and tried to laugh. "I guess not. Thank you, Jameson. It's perfect."

He replied quietly, "You're welcome."

They stared at each other, both realizing the animosity was gone, and now that it was, they both also realized they kind of liked each other.

CHAPTER NINETEEN

Ava walked up to her front door. It was late by the time she finally left the shop with her new tattoo. A bandage covered it, extending down along her hip. Digging into her purse for her keys, she didn't notice the vandalism until she was on the porch and reached out to slip the key in the lock. She gasped as she took in her door.

Spray painted in bright red was the word *SLUT*.

Ava's eyes immediately darted all around her, searching for someone watching. Who could have done this? Was it that crazy girl who was stalking Jameson, the one who threw the drink in her face? Ava could see this being her style. Or maybe that scary biker who she'd seen on the corner and had approached her car. But somehow, she just couldn't picture him bothering with graffiti. He seemed more like the type who'd show up at her door when she was home, not scrawl a vulgar message on it.

What about Dr. Ashton? He'd seemed to go off the deep end when she had replaced him. He'd reacted so angrily. Was he capable of something like this? Her mind went in a thousand directions, trying to figure out who would have done this.

She glanced around again and then hurried inside.

Once in, she slammed the door and threw the deadbolt. Leaning back against the wood, she flipped the lights on and scanned the room. She didn't see anything out of the ordinary, and it was dead quiet. Pulling her cell from her bag, she dialed her sister.

"Hey, Ava. How was work tonight?" her sister's bright cheery voice came through the earpiece.

"Steffy, someone vandalized my front door."

"What? How?"

"They spray-painted the word *slut* in bright red."

"Oh, my God. Did you call the police?"

"I just got home."

"Come over here. I don't want you there alone. I mean it, Ava."

"I'm fine."

"Do you know who did it?"

"I have a couple of ideas."

"I'm coming over, and we're talking about this. I'll be there in five minutes."

"You don't need to do that."

"Yes, I do."

Five minutes later, Ava opened the door when she heard her sister pull up and waited on the porch. Steffy walked up with a bag containing a gallon of ice cream. She was in sweat pants, flip-flops, and a baggy shirt, her hair up in a twist.

"Holy shit," she commented, taking in the vandalism.

"I know. It's bad. Come on, get inside."

"We can paint it tomorrow," Steffy offered as she followed Ava in, heading straight to the kitchen table to sit down.

Ava sat across from her with two spoons, tucking her foot under her butt. Passing one spoon to her sister, Ava scooped up a spoonful of ice cream direct from the carton.

"So spill. Who do you think did it?"

Ava told her about the three she'd come up with.

Steffy pulled her spoon from her mouth, frowning. "Wait a minute... back the train up. How come you didn't tell me about this biker or this stalker chick?"

"I didn't want you to worry." Ava avoided her eyes, her spoon going back for more.

"Well, newsflash, now I'm worried," Steffy bit out, her brows arched.

Ava stabbed her spoon in the gallon and left it

there, gazing toward the window. "I hate not knowing who it is. Now I'm going to be suspicious of everyone who looks sideways at me."

Steffy pointed her spoon at Ava. "It has to be someone you pissed off. I think you're right; it's one of those three. But do you really think Dr. Ashton would stoop to something like that? I mean, he's never struck me as the vindictive type."

Ava's eyes moved to her. "You didn't see how pissed he was the other night. It was like I had personally slighted him. He was acting like a scorned lover, which is ridiculous."

"That is so weird." Steffy made a face, taking another spoon of ice cream.

"I know, right?"

Steffy waved her spoon in the air, moving her head back and forth. "You just never know about people. The most mild-mannered can be the most screwed up in the head."

CHAPTER TWENTY

The next evening, Ava walked into the break room after the shop had closed. The brothers were sitting around drinking a beer. Max had one waiting for her on the table and held the ice-cold bottle out to her.

"Here you go, doll. Sit with us." He pulled the chair out next to him.

Ava took the bottle and sat, dropping her purse to the floor. She'd brushed aside their offers to have a beer with them so many times that she felt she had to accept. They were a fun-loving group she was quickly becoming attached to—Max with his protectiveness, Liam with his carefree joking, and Rory with his love of music. And the thought of going home to paint her door wasn't something she was looking forward to. Maybe she'd put it off until tomorrow morning.

"There's gonna be a meteor shower tonight," Liam informed the group as he sat straddled backward on his chair.

"Really, what time?" Max asked as he leaned back and draped his arm across Ava's chair.

"Yeah, I'm not staying awake all night to see it," Jameson added, tipping his bottle up for a drink.

"Supposed to start in about an hour and last until dawn," Liam replied.

"It's a clear night. Should be able to see some of it from the house," Rory observed.

Max turned to Ava. "Have you ever seen one?"

"I haven't."

"Come on out with us. You might be able to see some before it gets too late."

Her eyes immediately moved to Jameson, wondering if he would want her at his family home. His reception hadn't been that welcoming the last time she'd visited. But that was before things had started to thaw between them.

"You should come," he stated, washing away her trepidations.

"Yeah, we can get some more beer, build a bonfire… It'll be a good time," Max suggested, looking to her for a reply.

"All right. That sounds like fun."

***

An hour later, they lay around a bonfire, staring at the sky.

"I can't see shit this close to the fire," Max

announced.

"Me, either," Ava agreed.

Jameson climbed to his feet and extended his hand to her. "Come on. You can see better from over on that slope." He lifted his chin to an area toward the back of the property. She glanced over then slid her hand in his, and he pulled her to her feet.

The two of them trudged to the top with Ava hanging onto Jameson's hand for balance. They sat and lay back, staring at the sky.

Jameson rolled his head toward her. "You having a good time?"

She met his gaze. "Yes, I am. Your brothers are a hoot."

He again studied the sky, and his mouth pulled up as he answered sarcastically, "Yeah, they're a riot."

She giggled, and the melodic sound had him turning to smile at her.

"You can pretend all you want that they get on your nerves, but I know you love them."

"Do you?"

"Um hmm. You're all so close," she whispered.

He turned his attention back to the sky. "We've had to be."

She nodded, studying his somber expression from

the side. "It wasn't easy for you, was it?"

He rolled his head toward her again. "What wasn't easy?"

"Holding your family together."

He studied her a long moment, and then turned back to the stars. "It's all I've thought about for longer than I can remember."

"Do you ever worry that things may change?"

"How so?"

"Well, they're adults now with their own lives to lead, and one day that may take them in different directions." When Jameson didn't respond, she glanced over and asked, "Does that scare you?"

"It scares the crap out of me."

She looked at the stars, and they both lay quietly for a few minutes.

"My sisters and I, we lost our parents, too." Out of her peripheral vision she saw his head roll toward hers, but he remained silent. Finally, she turned to meet his gaze.

"I'm sorry," he offered softly.

She nodded.

"How?"

"Mom died of an aneurism. A year later, Dad died of a heart attack." She studied him. "Want to know a secret? I think he died of a broken heart. He was devastated when he lost her. I literally watched him deteriorate before my eyes."

"How old were you?"

"Twenty-two."

"Wait. You said sisters, *plural*. I didn't realize there were more than just you and Steffy."

She stayed quiet for a moment and felt her throat close up.

"Ava? You have more sisters?"

"Had."

"Had?"

"My youngest sister got sick not long after Dad died. The name of the disease is so long I can barely pronounce it." She knew her eyes were starting to glaze with tears, that he could see it happening. She tried to blink them away.

"She passed?"

Ava nodded. "I tried to save her. Did everything I could. And she fought so hard." She paused blowing out a breath, then shrugged. "None of it mattered in the end. I couldn't save her, and I carry that with me every day."

"I'm so sorry, Ava."

She nodded, wiping her tears on the sleeve of the

sweat jacket that Max had given her against the chilly night air.

"What was her name?"

She tried to smile. "Lily."

He rose up, resting his weight on his hand as he leaned over her. His eyes searched hers and then dropped to her hip. "Your tattoo?"

She nodded. "Yes. It was for her."

"Babe, why didn't you tell me?"

She shook her head. "I couldn't. I probably never would have said anything if you hadn't just asked."

He cocked his head to the side. "This Gala, the charity, is it for her?"

She wiped at her cheek again and huffed out a short, sniffled laugh. "Yes."

He dropped his head, growling, "Shit, I feel like such a dick."

"You didn't know."

He looked off toward the bonfire. "I didn't make it easy for you to tell me, though, either."

"No, you didn't."

He heard the smile in her voice, found her grinning through her tears.

"I guess we have more in common than I thought," he replied softly.

"I guess so."

"Tell me about the charity."

"I established it in my sister's honor because I felt I had to do something. There was just so much guilt."

"Guilt?" He frowned down at her.

She nodded. "Because I couldn't help her, because I failed her. Which is why I'll feel so guilty if the charity event is not successful. It'll be like I'm failing her all over again."

"I'm sorry." He looked off toward the bonfire. "I know what that kind of guilt can feel like. Like somehow you're to blame for all of it."

She studied his face. He'd felt it too, when he'd been struggling to keep his family together. "Jameson, you won with your brothers. But I lost with my sister."

His eyes returned to hers. "Babe, that's not true. What happened with your sister… That's not on you."

She turned her head away. "Isn't it?"

"Look at me." He cupped her jaw. "It's not your fault. You hear me?"

She studied his expression and the sincerity reflected there. Finally, she nodded.

After a long moment, he backed off, lied down beside her, and they both stared up at the stars. Two meteors in quick succession shot across the sky, their tails burning out almost immediately. They lay quietly, taking in the show the heavens put on for them. After a few moments, his hand slid over the few inches that separated them, and his fingers interlaced with hers.

"What a pair of broken toys we are," she murmured.

"Are you broken?" he asked softly, not looking at her.

"Probably." She turned her head. "Are you broken?"

He met her eyes and grinned. "Probably."

CHAPTER TWENTY-ONE

The next morning, Jameson sat at his desk, sipping coffee and watching the sun climb the eastern sky from the second floor window that overlooked Main Street. The steam rose from his mug as he stared off at the distant mountains on the horizon, just visible over the rooftops.

His mind dwelled on the things he and Ava had talked about last night. Her life paralleled his in so many ways. They both were the oldest taking care of younger siblings. They'd both lost parents. They'd both worked hard to build successful businesses they'd started on their own. They were both fighting to hold their families together. He grinned. And they both, quite possibly, had control issues.

Yet, as volatile as their relationship had begun, he was beginning to feel that somehow they may be the only ones to truly understand each other, and there was something calming about that. He thought about what she'd said about his brothers having their own lives that may take them in other directions. It was his biggest fear—that somehow he would lose the hold that had kept his family together all these years, and losing it terrified him more than anything. He'd held onto this family of his for so long, he wasn't sure he knew any other way to be. She'd seen that and recognized it for what it was. And he'd seen in her the fact that she only lived for her sister's memory, for a charity that represented some failing she felt she had to make up for—a debt he knew she clearly didn't owe. The realization dawned on him that perhaps they both saw each other more clearly than they were able to see themselves.

He turned from the window at the sound of boot steps on the stairs. Max came up and crossed the room to plop down in one of the chairs across from him.

"You're here early," Max commented.

"I was going to say the same thing about you."

Max grinned, crossed one boot over his knee, and tapped his heel almost as if he was considering his words carefully before speaking.

Jameson narrowed his eyes. "You got something to say?"

Max met his gaze. "Yeah, I do."

"Then spit it out."

"This one's not riding out of town on the back of some guy's bike, Jamie."

Jameson frowned. "Where the fuck did that come from?"

"Ever since Crystal left, you've been a bear. And it's not just that. You're not happy. You haven't been since Crystal."

"That's bullshit."

"We both know it's not."

Jameson set his mug on the desk and stared down at it. Max was right. Since Crystal left, he'd been in a tailspin—pissed at the world, taking it out on everyone, thinking about the past… until lately. Until a mouthy, know-it-all blonde with legs that went on for days walked into his life and turned it on its head.

As if reading his mind, Max said, "You're alike, you two. Hell, she brings out the best in you. Don't let the best thing that ever walked through those doors slip through your fingers."

Jameson remained mute.

"Jamie, she has her own business, so you know she's not after your money. And she's hot as hell, so what's the fucking problem?"

"Max—" Jameson warned, but refused to answer

his question.

"She's sweet, smart, sexy, wants to help with the business, and for some reason she's taking all the shit you shovel her way and tossing it back at you. I'd say she's a keeper, and you better open your fucking eyes before it's too late."

"Stay the fuck out of my business, Max," Jameson said quietly to his desktop.

"You know I'm right. You want to be pissed, be pissed at me. You want to lie to me, go on, but be honest with yourself at least, because I would hate to see you blow this all to hell."

"You done?" Jameson snapped loudly, hating having his nose rubbed in it.

"Yeah, I'm done."

"Then get the fuck out!"

"I love you, Bro. You know that, don't you?" Max reminded him with a grin as he got to his feet.

Jameson looked up and snapped, "Someday you're going to get knocked on your ass by a woman, and I'm going to be there taking pictures."

Max chuckled as he left.

***

Liam looked up from his chair when Max came back downstairs. He'd heard the yelling and knew Max had been trying to talk some sense into Jameson. He grinned and asked, "How'd that go?"

"I'm guessing you heard."

"He figure out he's in love yet?"

Max grinned and nodded. "He is so fucking screwed."

***

Later that afternoon, Ava headed back to the supply room to check inventory. She flicked the switch in the back hall and nothing happened. She looked up to see the light was burned out. Frowning, she glanced to the front to see that Max, Liam, and Rory were all working on customers, so she decided to just change it herself. She'd just need to find a ladder to reach the fixture.

There was one leaning against the back wall of the utility closet, behind the mop and bucket and some other items. She began to shuffle everything out of the way, and then manhandled the eight foot aluminum stepladder a few inches. It wasn't that it was extremely heavy, but it was a bit awkward to maneuver. She tried walking the feet back and forth, but soon was backed up against the door that began to shut behind her.

A moment later, the door was pushed open, and she was pressed against the wall, wedged between the door and ladder. She let out a little squeal.

Jameson poked his head around the door. "What the hell are you doing?"

She pushed herself upright. "I was trying to change the light bulb in the hall. It's out."

He stepped into the small room, his body taking up what little space remained as he caught the weight of the ladder so it wouldn't tip over on her. "Move."

She had to try to squeeze between him and the door to get out. He stared down at her as her body pressed against him as she moved around the edge of the door. Then his other arm was over her head, grabbing the rest of the weight of the ladder. She inhaled his scent—it wasn't a heavy overpowering cologne, but perhaps a body wash he used, and that combined with his own man's scent was amazing. She didn't want to move away; she found herself wanting to stay right there and continue breathing him in. It was like she'd suddenly found some new drug and was instantly addicted. All this flashed through her brain in a moment's time, and then she mustered the strength to move away.

Once she was out of the way, he carried the ladder out and positioned it under the fixture.

"I've got it from here," Ava insisted, a little

flustered by the reaction she'd just had to him.

"Suit yourself." He stepped out of the way, but he didn't leave.

Ava grabbed up a box containing a replacement bulb from the top shelf in the closet and scrambled up the ladder. She set the box on the top rung and began unscrewing the dome of the light fixture, trying her best to ignore him, which was damned near impossible.

Jameson stood at the bottom of the ladder watching, which made her fingers fumble a bit on the screws and drop one of them. She carefully lowered the glass covering and balanced it on the top rung. Then she unscrewed the burned bulb and replaced it with the new. Now she just had to put the cover back up. Her arms were getting tired holding the heavy glass fixture over her head while she fumbled with the screws. Jameson handed them to her, one by one. As she looked down to reach for them, she noticed his eyes drop to the curve of her hip and the tattoo he'd done for her. With her arms over her head as she replaced the screws, her shirt rode up exposing it, as well as her new piercing. The way his eyes moved over her skin had her wobbling a bit, and she almost lost her balance. In an instant, she felt Jameson's hands grab her thighs, holding her steady.

"Careful, babe."

She swallowed, thinking how close she'd come to slipping off the ladder and dropping the fixture to the floor. She noticed Jameson's hold remained firm until she finished and was coming back down the ladder.

Once she'd descended, she turned to find him standing only a few inches from her. They stared at each other a moment, and her eyes couldn't help but drop to his muscular chest and arms.

"Thanks," she murmured.

"Your ink seems to be healing nicely."

Finding herself at a loss for words, she could only nod. Was that all he'd been studying, how well it was healing? Not the way the art curled around the curves of her body? She remembered his words when he'd put it on her, how sexy a tattoo curving over the hip could be. Did he find hers sexy?

"I'll get the ladder." He lifted his chin toward it.

"Right." She stepped out of the way, and he folded and hefted it like it weighed nothing. After he put it back and shut the closet door, he flicked the light switch. They both glanced up at the now bright hallway. Then she watched him turn and walk upstairs without another word.

What the hell was happening to her? She'd been so

affected by his nearness, but she wasn't sure he'd been affected at all.

CHAPTER TWENTY-TWO

It was Saturday evening, and as Ava took the payment from the last customer, she noticed there were no more waiting. She pulled up the schedule in the computer and saw that all the slots after 8:00 p.m. were blocked off. *What now, another bachelorette party?*

"We're closing the shop early tonight." Max closed the door after his customer left, then flipped the sign over and walked to her counter.

She frowned up at him. "Why?"

"Rory's band is playing tonight at the bar down the street. We're all going to go see them. You're coming, too, aren't you?"

"I guess I'd forgotten," she admitted.

"They're really good. You should come."

Liam walked up. "How 'bout you ask that hot sister of yours to join us?"

She rolled her eyes, laughing.

Max leaned his forearms on the counter and

grinned down at her. "Yeah, you gonna be a sweetheart and hook a brother up?"

She rolled her eyes again. "I'll see what I can do."

Liam reached over the counter, pulled the receiver from the telephone system and handed it to her with a grin. "Hurry up, then. We're heading over there in a few minutes."

She made the call and informed them that Steffy would meet them there.

"She's not one of those girls who take two hours picking out an outfit and doing her hair and makeup, is she?" Liam asked, his hands sliding into his pockets.

"Isn't that all women?" Max huffed out a laugh.

"Um, well…" Ava hated to break it to them, but Steffy did take a long time to get ready to go anywhere.

"Oh, Lord," Liam muttered, shaking his head as Rory walked up, his jacket in hand.

Ava chuckled. "What time are you going on stage, Rory?"

"We won't go on until 9:00 p.m. She's got some time yet." He glanced at the clock on the wall. "I've got to head over and start setting up. Gary, our drummer got word that Sonny Baker from RBI West Coast Recordings is supposed to come see us tonight. So, I'll see you all over there."

"Not *the* Sonny Baker?" Liam teased with a grin, not having a clue who in the world the guy was. Not that any of them did.

"Blow me," Rory bit back.

"Save us a table up front," Jameson put in as he came downstairs and walked up to join the others in the lobby.

Rory stopped in the doorway and looked back, grinning. "I'll see what I can do."

"You better do more than see!" Jameson shouted after him as he went out the door.

***

Two hours later, the five of them were all seated at a table up front—Jameson, Max, Liam, Ava, and Steffy. Ava had to admit, Rory's band, Convicted Chrome, was really good. Rory was an excellent guitar player, taking center stage for more than one solo. He sang the lead on several songs, and Ava thought his vocals were much better than the other band member who sang most of the songs. She'd leaned over to ask Jameson about it, and he'd told her the other member had started the band and Rory had been added to the lineup only last year.

As she sat back and watched, it was clear—to her at least—that Rory was the star of the show and outshone the other members. She imagined he had big things in his future.

Glancing over at Jameson, she saw the pride in his eyes, but she also saw a hint of something else. It was almost like he was watching his kid graduate and go off to college. He was going to have to let go of Rory, and he knew it. Rory had bigger things in store for him than working at the family business, even if he loved Brothers Ink as much as the others.

As she studied the emotion on Jameson's face, she realized it wasn't going to be easy for him when that time came.

She glanced around the rest of the table. Steffy was squeezed between Max and Liam, and they were both lavishing her with attention, hitting on her left and right.

Steffy, for her part, was enjoying every minute of it, laughing at the brother's jokes as they ribbed and tried to one-up each other.

The band took a short break, which allowed for conversation to be heard.

Jameson picked up the pitcher of beer that sat on the table, leaned over, and refilled Ava's glass, then filled the others. Max was the only one at the table not drinking. When Ava had asked why, he'd said it was because he was in training for an amateur fight.

"Thank you." She smiled at Jameson.

He winked at her as he set the pitcher back down. "You havin' a good time?"

"I'm having a blast. This is a fun place." Her eyes traveled around the bar. It was an old building that had once been a bank at the turn of the last century. The ceilings were high, the walls had been gutted down to the brick, and the floors were hardwood. There was a long vintage bar with a gorgeous carved mirror along one side, and across the large room was a stage for the band. The place was called, appropriately enough, *The Vault*.

"Yeah, the acoustics are great in here." He glanced around, and then met her eyes. "What do you think of Convicted Chrome?"

"They're amazing. Although I'm not much for heavy metal rock, I love the songs that Rory sings on. He's got a wonderful voice."

Jameson nodded. "Yeah. I think his talent is wasted with this bunch." He grinned over at her. "But don't tell him I said that."

She chuckled. "My lips are sealed."

"After this break is their last set. Sometimes Rory and the lead singer do an acoustic number for the last song. Depends how the crowd is."

Ava nodded. "I'd love to hear it." She glanced around. "Do you know which guy is the music producer he was talking about?"

"No. I've got no clue what he looks like. I saw Rory talking to somebody earlier when they took that last break, but hell, it's so crowded, I wasn't sure it was him."

"I hope he's here," she replied.

Jameson looked over her head at something and muttered, "Fucking hell."

Before she could turn around, she noticed Liam's and Max's eyes lift as well, and the vibe at the table suddenly went from fun-loving to tense in an instant.

"Hey, Jameson," Ava heard in a feminine voice that sounded familiar, but also sounded drunk. She twisted and found herself staring up at the girl who had thrown the drink at her.

"Rachel," Jameson bit out. "I told you, don't want you in my shop, don't want you calling, and I sure as hell don't want you thinking there's anything between us. Go away."

As Ava studied the girl, she swayed on her feet, and it became immediately apparent just how drunk Rachel was.

"You can't tell me what to do," she slurred out, swaying.

Ava's eyes dropped to the glass in the girl's hand and wondered if she was about to get another drink dumped on her. She heard Jameson's chair scrape across the wooden floor as he stood, and suddenly they were facing off one another from either side of her chair. *Oh, crap.*

She glanced across the table to see Steffy's eyes move from the girl to her and get big in a meaningful way that said, *who the hell is this?*

The glass crashed to the floor, shattering behind Ava's chair and then Jameson was grabbing Rachel by the forearms as she almost stumbled to the floor along with it.

"Oops," she said with a giggle. Then she leaned toward Jameson, trying to hang all over him. "Why have you been so mean to me, Jameson?"

"Maybe you should call her a cab," Max advised.

"I can drive myself," Rachel insisted, trying to pull from Jameson's arms, suddenly all indignant.

Liam stood and pulled Steffy to her feet. "Come on, angel. Let's go play darts."

"Max, take Ava home while I deal with this," Jameson said as he held Rachel up by the forearms.

"Yeah, sure. No problem." Max stood and took Ava's hand.

She glanced back at Jameson who held up the swaying woman. "Will you be okay?"

"I'll be fine. I've just got to make sure she gets home. Last thing I want is her making a scene when Rory's band is playing. It's a big night for him."

***

Max escorted Ava out the door and to his truck. Once they were outside, Ava realized just how good the cool night air felt after the crowded bar. She took a deep breath.

"Stalker girl strikes again," Max said, looking over at Ava. "Sorry your night had to end with that."

She smiled over at him. "That's okay. I was getting tired, anyway." She glanced back at the bar as Max held the passenger door open for her. "What about Steffy?"

Max grinned. "Liam will make sure she gets home. Don't worry."

She climbed up, and he shut the door. A moment later they were headed down Main Street.

"Max?"

"Yeah, babe."

"I don't mean this in the wrong way, but Steffy is

my sister. What I mean is, will Liam treat her right?"

Max looked over at her. "She'll be fine, darlin'. I promise. Liam's a good guy. He won't take advantage, if that's your worry."

She smiled. "Sorry. I'm a big sister. We worry."

"And she's your little chick, huh?"

She chuckled. "Something like that."

"Don't worry, Mama hen. Little chick will be fine."

"Thanks."

A light smattering of raindrops began to fall, and Max flicked on the wipers. After another moment, he looked over at her. "So, you and Jameson seem to be getting along better."

Her mouth formed a small smile, and she looked down. "Yes, I suppose so."

"I'm glad. You're good for him."

"Am I?" She met his eyes.

"Yes, ma'am. You're shaking him up, in a good way. It's what he needs."

"I don't know about that."

"You two have a connection. Don't try to deny it."

She looked out her window, listening to the sound of tires on wet pavement. "I suppose you're right. Our situations are similar. I feel that bond; I won't deny it."

"He feels it, too."

She turned back to him. "Does he?"

"Absolutely. And it scares the hell out of him."

"Why? I don't want anything from him. I'm not after him like some of these groupies from his TV show."

"I think he's afraid that bringing a woman into the mix will upset the balance. At least, that's what he's always been afraid of in the past. Nobody was going to come between us as a family, and nobody was going to tear us apart. Then, when he became successful…Well, now it's all about the money. He can spot a gold-digger from a mile away. Like that chick and Rory."

"And is he afraid I'll do something to come between all of you?"

Max shrugged. "Maybe not. But strong feelings, like the kind he's starting to feel, they can scare the hell out of a man."

"You sound like you speak from experience," she teased.

He chuckled. "I've had my turn at the heartbreak hotel."

"Not going back again?"

"Oh, hell yeah. When the right one comes along, definitely."

She laughed. "Ah yes, the elusive 'right one'."

"You ever come close?"

She looked at him. "Me? No. I've barely dated." She looked out her window, watching the raindrops slide down the glass. "I spent most of my time taking care of my sisters."

"Same with Jameson. He's spent his whole life taking care of all of us. We all look up to him. He's been driven to succeed, but he's done it on his own terms, by his own rules. We admire the success he's made of the place. We know the struggle it's been and what he had to give up. He put his own wants aside for the good of the business, for the good of the family he's struggled so long to keep together. All this time, that's been his one and only goal. Not fame, not fortune. That was never his goal."

"I see."

"Do you? He inspires us. We all want him to be happy—it's his turn. I want that for him. We all do."

She looked at him. "Someday he'll find it."

Max took his eyes from the road. "I think he already has. He just needs to figure it out, sweetheart."

She smiled and shook her head. "Ever the matchmaker, huh, Max?"

He chuckled. "A year from now, I'll remind you that you said that."

She laughed and directed him down the street to her house. A moment later, he was pulling in the drive. When he put it in park, she opened her door.

"Wait, I'll walk you up."

"There's no need. It's raining. I'll be fine."

"All right. I'll wait until you get inside."

"Thanks for the ride, Max."

"You're welcome, Ava."

She climbed out and dashed through the raindrops up the steps. Unlocking the door, she stepped in and turned to wave at him. He lifted his hand off the steering wheel, returning it.

She closed the door and turned to drop her purse on the floor.

That's when she saw him—the scary biker from Brothers Ink was sitting on her sofa in the dim light of the table lamp.

She whirled, grabbing for the door handle, hoping that Max was still in the drive, but he was on her in a flash, shoving her against the door and clamping his hand over her mouth.

"What's the matter, Princess? Aren't you glad to see me?" he hissed in his sinister voice.

She tried to turn her head, her mind frantic as she tried to think of a way to save herself. Her arm flung out feeling along the wall, and she felt the light switch that controlled the porch light. She frantically flicked it on and off repeatedly, hoping the biker wouldn't notice what she was doing.

***

Max backed out onto the street. As he cranked the wheel and shifted into drive, his eyes were drawn to the flickering porch light. He paused, frowning at the flashes. *What the hell?*

He pulled back up the drive, put the truck in park, and jogged up to the door. Immediately, he could hear the struggling coming from just inside. Pounding on the door, he shouted, "Ava! Ava, open the door."

He tried the doorknob, but it was locked. He pounded again. As he was contemplating which window to bust in, he heard the lock flip open. He grabbed the knob again and pushed inside.

Ava was leaning against the wall. Her shirt was torn, and she was sobbing.

"Where is he?" Max snapped.

She pointed toward an archway that led to a kitchen. He dashed through it. The back door was wide open. He ran out just in time to see a big black Harley in an alley behind her garage. The biker gunned it away in the rain, but not before turning to look at him.

Max couldn't make out his features, but he knew it was one of Ryder's crew by the insignia clearly visible on the back of his leather vest.

Max slammed the back of his fist into the doorframe as the roaring sound of the drag pipes faded into the distance. Then he went back inside and found Ava standing in the entryway to the kitchen.

"Are you okay?" he asked.

She nodded.

He moved to her and, taking her upper arms in his hands, drew her to the kitchen table and coaxed her down into a chair. He squatted in front of her. "Did he hurt you?"

She shook her head. "No. I'm okay. Thank God you came back."

"I saw the light. That was smart."

"It was all I could reach. He had me pinned to the door."

Max nodded. "You got any booze?"

She looked at him blankly, but nodded toward a cabinet. "Top shelf."

He moved to it and came back with a glass and a bottle of tequila. He poured her a shot and held it out to her. She looked up at him and downed it, making a face.

Max watched her closely. "Another?"

She shook her head.

He smoothed the hair on the top of her head. "I need to make a call. You sit tight, okay?"

"You're not calling the police, are you?"

"No, not the police." She stared up at him. He filled her glass and slid it toward her, disregarding her earlier reply, declining. "Be right back."

He moved into the living room, pulling his cell from his pocket, his thumb moving over the screen before he put it to his ear. It rang twice before Jameson picked up.

"Yeah?"

"I'm at Ava's. Brother, get over here, now. She was just attacked."

"What the fuck do you mean, she was attacked? Is she okay?"

"Yeah, just get here."

Less than five minutes later, they heard a motorcycle roar up. At Ava's panicked look, Max squeezed her hand. "It's only Jamie." She looked up at him questioningly as he stood. "Stay here."

***

Jameson barely took the time to drop his kickstand before jumping from his bike. He took the porch steps two at a time. The front door banged against the wall as he burst through. All he could think about was getting to Ava.

Max met him in the living room.

"Where is she?" Jameson demanded.

Max put his hands up. "Calm down. She's in the kitchen having a stiff drink. She's shaken up, but she's okay."

Jameson made to push past him, but Max put a hand to his chest holding him back. "It was one of Ryder's crew. She admitted he's been harassing her."

That had him stopping dead in his tracks as he felt his blood run cold. *"What?"*

Max nodded toward the front door.

Jameson twisted to look back at it, noticing for the first time the slanderous word. It looked like she'd tried to paint over it, but hadn't used a second coat and the shadow of the word still showed through. A sick feeling settled in the pit of his stomach.

"Didn't want to admit it. For some reason she's afraid you'll be mad."

Jameson's head swiveled back to Max, stunned, not believing what he was hearing. But he could see the reproach in the look Max was giving him, and he clenched his jaw.

"Ryder's' crew, that needs to be dealt with," Max growled.

Jameson nodded. "It will be, count on it. But not tonight. Tonight is just about Ava."

Max nodded in agreement. "I tried to get her to come back to the farm with me. She won't go."

Jameson pushed his hand off. "I've got this. Go home."

Max jerked his head toward the kitchen. "Don't leave her here alone tonight. Not with that guy on the loose. Not till we catch him."

"Not a chance. Now go."

"Jameson—"

"I've got her," he reassured.

Max nodded. "Okay."

Jameson walked in the kitchen, his eyes taking in Ava. "You okay?"

She nodded, but remained uncharacteristically quiet, and that scared the hell out of him. Jameson stared down at her bent head, his jaw clenching while he waited for the sound of the front door closing. The moment he heard it, he was down on his knee in front of her, a million emotions warring inside him—fear, anger, frustration...*and a ton of guilt*.

She put her face in her hands, but he wasn't about

to let her hide from him. He clasped her wrists, pulling them down. "Look at me, sweetheart."

He heard her whimper and sniffle, but she wouldn't look up, and those sounds gutted him. His voice was soft as he pleaded, "Please, Ava."

Finally that cute little chin of hers came up, and she stared at him with eyes glassy with tears. She tried to fake a tremulous smile. "I'm fine. I don't know why Max made such a fuss."

"Did he hurt you?" Jameson cut straight to the most important question on his mind.

She shook her head.

He studied her, wondering if he was getting the truth. "You can tell me."

"Can I?"

"Don't you know you can?"

She shook her head again. "No, I don't."

That had him pulling his chin back. The thought that she felt that way tore him up. "Why?"

"And give you another reason to throw in my face about how I'm not cut out for this job, and what a complaining princess I am? No way."

He stood at that, so taken aback by her words. "What the hell are you talking about? Is that really how you see me? And what the hell does any of this have to do with work? A man attacked you."

She stayed quiet.

"Max said it wasn't the first time this guy has bothered you."

"No."

"I saw the door. Babe, why the hell didn't you tell me?" When she stayed quiet, he pulled her out of the chair, his hands on her upper arms. His voice was soft, but determined. "Why didn't you tell me?"

She tried to pull out of his grip. "I didn't want to be any more trouble to you."

"I'm supposed to protect you."

She looked up at him with wide, confused eyes.

"You work for me. No man who comes in my shop is going to give a woman who works for me any trouble. Do you understand?"

She just stared at him.

"Ava?"

She looked away.

"Do you think I'd let anyone hurt you?"

She shook her head.

"Tell me what happened."

She shook her head again. "I can't."

He pulled her into his arms, cradling her head against his chest, his hand stroking her hair. "Please,

Ava. I need to know."

She spoke into his chest. "Max dropped me off. He wanted to walk me to the door, but it was drizzling and I told him that was silly. So he waited until I went inside."

"The guy... He was in the house?" He felt her head nod against his chest, and a wave of anger surged through him. Just the thought of someone breaking in and getting to her that way had his blood boiling. "What happened?"

She pulled back and looked at him. "He was sitting on the sofa. I'd left a small light on. I'd taken two steps into the house before I noticed him. It happened so fast. I tried to get to the door, but he was on me so quick. Before I could even scream, he had his hand over my mouth and pinned me against the door."

"You knew him? Recognized him?"

She nodded. "That biker who got the tattoo from Rory? It was his friend — the scary one who talked to me."

He closed his eyes, cursing, and then looked back at her. "I'm sorry. I swear to you, he won't ever bother you again."

"I was so afraid." She broke down crying, and he cradled her to him again. And then suddenly she was grabbing at his shirt, clutching him for dear life. His arms tightened around her, and he held her until she quieted.

"Shh, baby. You're safe now. I'm here."

He held her a long time.

"You want me to call your sister?"

She shook her head against his shoulder. "No, she'll worry. I don't want her to worry."

"Okay, honey. I won't call her."

Finally, she tilted her chin up to meet his gaze. He brushed the hair back from her face, searching her eyes. He wanted to offer up more reassurances, but as he stared down into her big blue eyes, words failed him. They stared at each other a long time, and there was a wave of silent communication moving between them. He cared about her; she had to see that. Surely it was written all over him.

And then he saw her gaze drop to his mouth, and he felt the room float away. She lifted the mere inches that separated their mouths. The brush of her lips was soft, gentle, which he allowed for about three seconds before he cradled her head in his hands and took control, deepening the kiss. He backed her into the nearest wall, and they kissed like two lovers who'd been parted for years, which was crazy, he knew, but he also knew it felt like exactly the right description.

Finally, he broke the kiss, pressing his forehead to hers, trying to regain his control. But she blew that all to hell with her next words.

"Don't stop." She clutched at him, trying to pull him back down. "Please. Don't stop."

"Ava—"

"Stay with me. Make love to me."

He stared down at her. "What?"

Her arms were around his neck already, and she tightened her hold. "Please. I need you, tonight. I don't want to be alone."

She needed him. For the first time since they met, she needed him, and not just to do the Gala or on some professional level, but on a personal level, the way a woman needs a man, and he liked how that made him feel. "I'm not going to leave you alone." He paused to shake his head. "Sex doesn't have to be part of it, Ava."

"Don't you want me?"

He frowned down at her, brushing her hair back. Of course he wanted her, he hadn't wanted a woman this much in a long fucking time. But he didn't admit any of that to her. Instead, he asked a question of his own. "You're sure?"

She nodded, her mouth coming up to claim his

again.

He didn't hesitate. He was done fighting whatever it was that flared to life whenever they were within ten feet of each other. He couldn't ignore it anymore, and he wouldn't want to if he could. It was there, burning brightly, refusing to be denied. Perhaps it had been there all along, since the day he'd stormed into her office with that damned flyer. Hell, one day he may just frame that damned flyer.

He hoisted her up, her legs naturally wrapping around his waist as he growled, "Which way?"

She knew what he was asking. "Through the living room."

He carried her out of the kitchen, through the living room, and to the back hallway. He passed a bathroom and entered the door at the end of the hall. He didn't bother with the light, but carried her to the queen bed he saw outlined in the shadows. He took her down to the mattress, coming down on top of her.

She tore at his t-shirt until he was lifting off her to rip it over his head. He sat up fumbling with his belt, and she pulled her shirt over her head. He moved off her to undo the fastening of her jeans and yank them down her long legs. Then he crawled back up her body, his hands gliding over skin smooth as silk.

Her back arched as her hands slid under herself, fumbling with the closure of her bra. He glided a hand under her, knocking her fingers out of the way to do the job himself, snapping it open with a flick. Then he pulled the garment free to toss to the floor with the growing pile of discarded clothing. He stared down at her, taking in her beauty in the starlight coming in through the curtains.

Her arms wrapped around him, pulling him down. "Take me. Hard. Fast."

There was that urgency again. It was almost like she thought he'd reconsider and change his mind. *No chance in hell, baby doll.* To prove to her just how remote that possibility was, his hand reached down and curled around the scrap of lace at her hip, and with one swift tug, he tore it from her body. It got the reaction he was looking for. Her eyes widened, and she sucked in a gasp.

Then he reached down freeing himself from his jeans and positioned himself between her thighs. He stared into her eyes. "You sure?"

"Yes. *God, yes*. Please."

He thrust into her in one quick movement, and then held himself poised above her. She stared up into his face with big luminous eyes. "Tell me you want me, too."

"Can't you feel how much?" He thrust his hips, driving his point home. "This has been a long time coming, hasn't it?

"Yes," she panted. "Again."

He complied, sliding slowly out and then thrusting back in.

"Again. Harder. Show me."

He nodded. "I'll show you." And he began to take control, increasing his pace and the power behind his driving motions until she was pushing with both palms against her headboard to keep from being driven up by his powerful body.

When he noticed, his forearm slid under her back, he pulled out, rose up on his knees and with one swift jerk, flipped her to her stomach. Then that arm yanked her up to on all fours as he got back into position and thrust home again.

Her mouth flew open, and she moaned.

His palm landed between her shoulder blades as he pushed her chest to the bed. Then his hands clamped around her hips and held her pinned while he powered into her.

"You like this?" His words were sharp, his breathing heavy with exertion.

"Yes. Don't stop," she gasped out, her fists curling into the coverlet.

He took one big palm and smoothed it tenderly over her ass, the small of her back, and then up her spine as he continued to glide in and out. His eyes moved over the edges of the tattoo he'd put on her as it peeked around her side. His gaze wandered up all the untouched skin of her back, and he thought of all the art he'd like to put there. "Beautiful. Do you know how beautiful you are?"

She moaned. "Jameson."

He slid his hand up the nape of her neck, his fingers threading into her hair, his fist closing around a handful to pull her head back slightly. "Do you know?"

"Tell me," she said breathlessly.

"So fucking beautiful."

He was getting close. He could feel it. But he wanted her there with him. He released her hair. His arm moved around her, his fingers dipping into her wetness and sliding it all over her, finding just the right motion and tempo that had her frantic with need. Then he changed the angle of his thrusts slightly.

"Yes. *There*," she told him, her palms going to the headboard and her head burying in the coverlet.

His breath was sawing in and out with his

exertions. "You're so fucking hot, Ava. I want you to come all over my dick. Will you do that, baby?"

She moaned, nodding and thrusting her ass up higher, meeting every slam of his hips. His fingers drew the motions out until she was bucking against his hand. He had her hovering on the edge, and then over she went with a cry. He felt her wetness all over his dick as he plunged into her again and again. He clamped both hands around her hipbones as he powered into her until one final slam, and he exploded with his own orgasm.

His hand planted in the mattress by her head as he leaned over her, his breathing sawing in and out as he let his weight drop down on top of her. Both palms glided along the coverlet as he rested on his elbows, boxing her in, his mouth nuzzling at her ear. "You good?"

He could hear the smile in her voice as she replied. "More than good."

Her palms slid over his hands as his mouth suckled at her throat.

"I didn't even get a chance to play with your tits," he teased.

She giggled, and he felt the vibration through her back. "Next time."

He nipped at her skin. "Definitely next time." Then he pressed a soft kiss to the spot.

She sighed.

He pulled out and moved back off her.

"Don't go," she moaned.

He smacked one ass cheek. "Pack a bag."

She twisted to look back at him as he stood at the foot of her bed, fastening his jeans and belt. "What? No."

"Not joking, Ava. Pack a bag."

"For what?"

"You're coming with me to the farm."

"I can't do that."

His brow arched. "Pack a fucking bag, Ava. Or so help me, I'll take you out of here without a stitch."

She rose up, glaring at him and knelt, sitting on her heels. "Are you serious?"

"As a heart attack." He moved to the side of the bed, took her face in his hands, and pulled her up for a kiss. He felt her arms wrap around his waist and her breasts press against his bare chest, hot skin on hot skin.

When he broke the kiss, her head still in his hands, she shifted her eyes and looked down at the bed. "Did that really just happen?"

He took one of her hands in his and held it against his chest. "You feel my heart still pounding? That's real, and yes, that really just happened."

"Stay here with me," she purred. "Please."

"As sweet as it is hearing your sexy voice beg, we're going."

"I'm staying here."

She tried to push out of his arms, but he wouldn't let her. He stared down into her face and clarified in a gentle voice, "What happened to you tonight... I'm pissed off and feeling protective. Don't push me on this, Ava. It's happening. Understand?" He knew she saw the rock solid determination to have his way in his expression, and for once, she backed down. "Good girl." He kissed her nose. "Now grab enough for a few days."

"*Days?*"

"Yes, no arguments now." She climbed off the bed, but wasn't quick enough before he smacked her ass again. "Move, woman."

"Ow."

"And it's gotta fit in my saddlebags, so don't over-pack."

Her hands landed on her hips. "I don't have a bag that will fit in your saddlebag, Jameson."

He grabbed up her pillow, yanked the pillowcase off, and tossed it to her. "Problem solved."

She rolled her eyes, chuckled, and headed to her closet. "You're unreal."

"Think I just proved to you how very real I am, babe."

He heard giggling coming from the closet, followed by a low, murmured, "You certainly did."

He grinned.

CHAPTER TWENTY-THREE

An hour later, with Jameson's firm grip on her hand, Ava was led through the big, dark farmhouse to his bedroom. Maybe she'd never admit it, but that firm grip — and the way he'd come over and taken control tonight — was exactly what she needed.

She followed him into the room. It was on the second floor, with a huge window overlooking the view. He let go of her hand, and she walked to the window. A full moon shone down on the valley with the mountains in the distance.

He came to stand behind her and wrapped his arms around her waist. "I meant what I said."

"What's that?" She turned her head to the side, and he nuzzled her ear.

"You don't have to worry about that guy again. I'll take care of it. I'll take care of you. No matter what, be it that guy or Rachel or anyone else who threatens you. Understand?"

"Okay." He'd never know how much that meant to her.

"You and me, we've been at cross purposes from the start. I just think we don't understand each other, but that's gonna change tonight." His arms tightened. "Can I tell you something?" he asked.

She nodded.

"I like this feeling."

"What feeling?"

"You needing me," he confessed.

"Can I tell you something?" she whispered back.

"Anything." His voice was deep and rumbly in her ear.

Her hand came up to hold his cheek to hers. "I liked you taking control. I like having someone to lean on. Even if it's only for the night."

This was a pivotal turning point in their relationship, and they both realized it. Things were changing between them.

He stepped back, taking her hand and drawing her back with him. He stopped next to the bed, and his hands lifted to her blouse, his fingers working the buttons free. She lifted her hand and traced a tattoo that ran down his arm.

His eyes followed the motion, and then lifted to

hers.

She smiled. "I've wanted to do that for the longest time."

"I wish I'd known that. Maybe we would have gotten to this point a whole lot sooner."

Her eyes dropped back to the tattoo.

"I'll let you trace every one of them if you want, babe."

She grinned. "I'll take you up on that."

"But not right now. I've got something else in mind." He reached the last button of her blouse and pulled the placket open. Their eyes held as he pushed it back off her shoulders. "We rushed this earlier. I want to take my time with you."

He slowly undressed her piece by piece and then, true to his word, he took his time, lavishing every part of her body with attention. His mouth moved over her skin from her mouth to her neck, to her breasts. He gave them extra time, reminding her with a teasing voice that he'd neglected them the first go around.

When he had her moaning and writhing, he moved on down her belly. He paused, giving special attention to the tattoo that curved over her hip. It had been several weeks since he'd given it to her, and it was now completely healed. She watched as his head dipped, and he traced along the edge with his tongue, following it over the curve of her hip and back up to her last rib. Then he dove straight for her bellybutton, his tongue toying with her new piece of jewelry.

He grinned up at her. "Look at you, my little wild thing, all pierced and tatted." He put his mouth back to her skin, his tongue drawing a pattern.

She trembled at his tickling touch, and he lifted his head, his eyes connecting with hers. The sexual heat burning in his eyes had her writhing beneath him. It didn't take him long to get the hint, and a sexy grin split his mouth as he slid lower. "Don't worry, baby. We've got all night, and I plan to see you're well taken care of." Then he grinned that Cheshire grin. "Repeatedly."

He slid lower and his mouth closed over her. Her head went back at the sensation of his tongue gliding over her again and again. His big hands pushed her thighs apart as his shoulders moved between them, spreading her wide and open to him. He took his sweet time, bringing her to one orgasm that stretched into another, until she was begging him to take her.

He slid up over her body, his knees pushing her thighs open, and thrust into her in one powerful move. She gasped, and his mouth closed over hers, silencing any noise but her moan of pleasure. His big body began to move, and her arms slid up his back, clutching him to her. She felt the muscles rippling beneath her palms as his skin grew damp with sweat.

His pace increased as he drove into her, slam after slam until she was bucking beneath him. His eyes held hers, and then he took her wrists, pulling her arms from around his neck to press them into the pillow on either side of her head. His fingers laced with hers.

"This means something, Ava. *You* mean something."

His body kept on thrusting as they stared into each other's eyes.

"Jameson." Her head went back, and she felt his mouth latch onto her throat, and still he kept thrusting furiously. His mouth moved to her ear.

"I'm gonna come. You want it?"

"Yes," she moaned.

His hands tightened around hers, and a moment later he drove into her, and his body went rigid. His breathing was heavy in her ear, and then he was slowly gliding in and out. Once. Twice. He collapsed down on top of her.

She could feel his chest moving as his breath rasped in her ear. She smiled, wrapping her arms around him and holding him close. He'd opened up a whole new side of himself tonight, and she reveled in it. It had taken them so long to get here, to this place where all the walls were broken down. Finally being here with him meant all the more to her.

She felt him start to pull away, and her arms tightened, stopping him. She turned her head, her lips pressing kisses down the side of his jaw, across to his ear. She whispered, "Don't go. Don't move."

She felt his weight settle back down, and his hips flexed. She grinned feeling him still hard inside her and moaned. He must have heard the smile in her voice, for he lifted his head to grin down at her. "Goddamn, girl."

She chuckled and dug her heels into his ass cheeks. "What?"

"You want round two, it's gonna take me a minute."

She reached down and smacked his ass. "Round three. You're losing count."

His brows shot up, and his hands closed over her wrists, pinning her again. "You lookin' to get rough, I can spank an ass, too."

She burst out laughing and wiggled her body. "Guess that would kill a minute or two while we wait."

She felt his body shake with his laughter as he

rolled and took her up on her offer.

***

Hours later, they watched the moon rise through the window. He lay behind her with his elbow in the pillow and his head in his hand. Her back was to his chest and his other arm was around her waist.

"You feel safe here?" His mouth nuzzled her head.

Her hand came up to touch his forearm. "Very safe."

He pressed a kiss to her temple. "Good. I want to talk."

She frowned, staring out the window at the moon. "What about?"

"Before tonight, what other encounters have you had with this guy?"

She stroked his forearm again as he waited patiently for her to answer. "He was standing outside near the shop one night when I left. I got stuck at the corner light."

"What happened?"

"He approached my car. Rapped on the driver's window. Scared the crap out of me."

"What did you do?"

"The light changed, and I drove off."

"Did he follow?"

She shook her head. "No. But one night a motorcycle followed me home. I don't know for sure, but I think it was him. He drove on down the street. At the time I thought I was being silly and paranoid."

"Did you ever see him near your house?"

"No."

"When did the vandalism of your door happen?"

"The other night. I came home after work, and it was there."

"Anything you're not telling me?"

"No. That's it." She paused. "Well, I did have one other visitor." She felt his body go tense behind her.

"Who?"

"Before you, there was another man who was going to be our headlining bachelor. When he found out he'd been replaced, he came over one night to confront me."

"What happened?"

"He was just angry. Told me I could forget about his help with the charity from then on."

"Who is this guy? What's his name?"

"Jameson—"

"Who is he?" he snapped.

"His name is Dr. Ashton. He's a surgeon here in town."

Jameson was quiet.

"You're not going to do anything are you?"

"Nobody messes with you, Ava. Told you that."

"He's harmless, Jameson."

"No man is harmless, Ava. Don't ever forget that."

"Now you're scaring me again."

He pressed a kiss to her head. "Sorry. Get some sleep, babe."

He settled in behind her, pulling her against his body, and she welcomed the embrace, loving the way he held her close and the heat of his skin on hers.

"Can I tell you something?" she whispered.

"Anything, babe."

"When I first laid eyes on you, I was so drawn to you."

He chuckled. "Could've fooled me."

"Shush. I'm being serious."

"Sorry, proceed."

"You push me to do things I wouldn't normally do… to see things in a different light. You make me excited about things I didn't know I would be excited about. You live your life on your own terms. There's something very appealing about that."

He was quiet a moment and then said, "Just don't ever let me push you too far, Ava. Promise?"

"I promise."

He kissed her temple. "Get some sleep, angel."

Eventually, they both drifted off.

***

Hours later, Ava woke up. She glanced at the illuminated time on the bedside clock. *4:00 a.m.* Jameson was curled around her with his arm slung over her waist, his hand splayed against her belly.

She could get used to this; She loved the feel of his hard body behind her, the protective pose, his body heat warming her and the comforting sound of his rhythmic breathing soothing her back to sleep.

She never thought she could feel this way with him—so relaxed and content. Not with the man who'd fought her and pushed her and driven her mad all these weeks. Yet here she was, lying in his arms, happier than she could remember being. She didn't want this to end. She didn't want this magical moment to *ever* end—Jameson pressed up against her, no fights or problems or worries, no bets or dares or games between them.

She squeezed Jameson's arm still wrapped around her, and even in his sleep, he moved in tighter. She smiled. Heaven… right here on earth.

CHAPTER TWENTY-FOUR

Jameson stood in the kitchen, leaning back against the sink under the window, a mug of coffee in his hand, a pair of dark gray sweats hanging low on his hips. He sipped the hot brew, thinking about last night and how things had changed between himself and Ava. He'd never in a million years have guessed they'd have the sexual chemistry that had flared between them last night. It was off the charts hot.

In the light of day he couldn't help thinking maybe it was a line he shouldn't have crossed. He was her boss, after all. How would that look? And here he'd gone on to her when they first met about how he didn't date women who worked for him. Made a point of it. Last night sure made a liar out of him.

They'd had a deal. This arrangement was supposed to be temporary. Nothing more. He'd get his parking spots, and she'd get a headliner for her Gala. He'd get what he wanted; she'd get what she wanted. Nothing was ever supposed to come of this. He wasn't supposed to start liking her. He wasn't supposed to start caring about her. But as he'd watched her sleep this morning, he couldn't help but think... *She's changing everything.*

Liam came in and moved to the coffee pot. As he poured himself a mugful, his eyes shifted to Jameson. "Max told me what happened last night. She okay?"

"Yeah, just shook up. She's okay now. You get her sister home okay?"

Liam nodded as he returned the carafe to the burner and turned toward him. Leaning one hand on the edge of the counter, he brought the mug to his lips. With it poised to drink, he added, "Heard it was one of Ryder's crew. How're we gonna handle that?"

"We?"

"We're brothers, right? Got each other's backs don't we? And we all like Ava. She shouldn't have to deal with this shit. Not because of our shop."

"She shouldn't have to deal with blowback on anything to do with Brothers Ink."

Liam took a sip. "Agreed. So what's the plan? We come down on anyone in that club, we'll have the whole lot on us."

"I'll deal with it."

"The hell you will. Not alone."

Jameson shook his head. "I'll deal with Ryder. He'll deal with the problem."

"You sure about that?"

"Absolutely. Ryder likes his ink—our shop, specifically. We've done all his work, haven't we? I doubt he's gonna let this bullshit fuck that up. Besides, she sits on the city council. Any shit goes down with her, that's media attention he *does not* want. I guarantee."

"You dealing with him today?"

"He's out of town till the end of the week."

"Ava lives alone, from what Steffy told me. You gonna keep her out here till then?"

"She's got a stubborn streak. That may be a problem."

Liam chuckled. "Hmm, who does that remind me of?"

"Shut the fuck up, asshole," Jameson replied with a grin.

"So how you gonna protect her if she won't stay?"

"I figure I can keep her here at least until Monday or Tuesday."

"And then?"

"I got that trip I've got to make to Denver. Guess she's goin' with me."

Liam huffed out a laugh. "How're you gonna pull that off?"

"It's business. I'll just make her go."

His brother chuckled again. "Right. I'll buy a ticket to see that show."

Jameson shoved his shoulder.

Max came in, and having heard the end of their conversation, added, "I don't think Jamie will have any trouble convincing her." He grinned over at Jameson. "Walls are thin, Bro."

"Christ," Jameson muttered, shaking his head. Then his eyes drilled into Max's. "You say anything to her, you're dead."

"I wouldn't dream of embarrassing the lady." He put his hands up in surrender. "You, on the other hand, are a different story." He dropped his arms and made a thrusting motion.

Jameson threw a paper towel roll at him, wooden stand and all. The roll came loose, rebounded off Max's bicep and bounced to the floor. He tried to make a grab for it and came up with the wooden dowel holder. He promptly moved to Jameson and wrestled him into a chokehold with it as Liam dodged out of the way, attempting not to spill his coffee.

At that moment, Ava walked into the kitchen with

Rory.

"Rut row," Rory said in his best Scooby Doo voice.

"Good morning, beautiful," Liam greeted her, moving to put an arm around her shoulders as they watched the two men wrestling.

"Good morning," she murmured, taking in the show as the men roughhoused, bouncing from cabinet to cabinet.

"Can I get you a cup of Joe?" Liam offered with a grin over the scuffling noise.

Jameson finally shoved Max off. "Knock it the hell off, dickhead. There's a lady present."

"Yeah, there is, so watch the cursing, Brother," Max reminded him as he straightened his black tank top. Then he moved to Ava, taking her face in his hands to gently press a kiss to her cheek. "How are you, sweetheart?"

Jameson took in both Liam with his arm around her shoulder and Max kissing her cheek and said, "Quit pawing all over her. Both of you."

Max stepped back and gave Jameson a look. "What crawled up your ass this morning?"

"Language."

"Oops. Right. Sorry, doll."

Ava looked up at Liam. "Did you take Steffy home

last night?"

"Yes, ma'am. Dropped her off, walked her to the door." He paused to look at Rory, a big grin on his face. "And got a kiss goodnight."

"You suck," came Rory's reply to that.

Liam chuckled.

"That's okay," Rory continued. "I hear she likes guitar players." He looked meaningfully at Ava.

Liam's eyes moved between them. "Not for long. When she saw the mob of groupie chicks around the stage, she told me no man was worth standing in line for."

"Blow me."

"Who's cooking breakfast?" Jameson asked, putting an end to their squabble. All their eyes swung to Max.

"Okay. Guess that would be me," Max replied. He gave Ava a wink. "I make a mean omelet. You like omelets?"

She grinned back. "Love them."

***

After breakfast, the brothers made themselves scarce, leaving Jameson and Ava alone. Jameson moved to the sink, dumped the dregs of his coffee, and turned back to Ava. "You want more coffee?"

She sat at the breakfast table, her chair turned toward where he stood at the sink, and shook her head. "Can you take me back to my car?"

Jameson frowned at her. Today was Sunday and the shop was closed. "Can't we pick it up tomorrow when we go in to work?"

She didn't answer.

Then he noticed her glancing at the calendar and fidgeting with her hands. "Ava? You have somewhere you need to be today?"

She nodded.

He came to stand over her. When she finally looked up at him, he said, "I'll take you anywhere you need to go, just tell me."

She looked down at her hands. "Today's the seventeenth."

His eyes hit the calendar, and then dropped back to her. "What's the seventeenth?"

"Lily's birthday. I usually put flowers on her grave." Her big eyes lifted to him.

He nodded. "Okay. Then we'll put flowers on her grave. We can leave whenever you're ready."

She stood and kissed his cheek. "Thank you."

He longed to be a source of strength for her. He liked that she'd leaned on him last night. He'd liked that she'd needed him. He wanted to take it further. He wanted her to depend on him. The fact that he had those feelings made him realize just how deep his feelings for her were beginning to go.

He watched her walk up the stairs, and he thought about how she was beginning to wrap around his heart without even trying.

***

An hour later, they were in his truck heading across town. Jameson turned toward Ava. "Have you talked to Steffy?"

"Briefly this morning. She's meeting me at the cemetery."

"Did you tell her about last night?"

"No." She looked at him sharply. "I don't want her to know, Jameson."

"Always the big sister, huh? Protecting the rest, even when its you that needs the support and protection."

She stared out the window. "I'll be fine. I just… I just don't want her to worry. What purpose would it serve?" She turned back to him. "I mean it. She doesn't need to know."

He took his attention from the road to search her eyes, thinking there was more he wanted to say. In the end, he gave in. "Fine. She won't hear it from me."

She looked back out the window. "Thank you."

He pulled his truck down the curving drive of the cemetery she'd directed him to. He came to a stop where she indicated. It was overcast with a light drizzle falling. His intermittent wipers swishing across the windshield was the only sound in the quiet cab of the truck.

The cemetery was beautifully kept with rolling grassy areas nestled amid majestic trees. He got out of the truck and went around to help her down. She had a bunch of flowers they'd stopped and purchased gathered in her arms. He followed her silently through the headstones until she finally stopped at one.

Ava brushed some leaves and pine needles off the top of the stone and laid the flowers across it.

Jameson stood watching, giving her all the space and time she needed.

She stared at the gravestone a long time and then whispered so softly, he almost didn't hear. "How do you move past a loss like this?"

Her eyes turned to his, looking for an answer he didn't have. "I don't know, Ava. I think you just have to go on living. It's what she'd want."

A few minutes after they arrived, the sound of

another vehicle drew their attention. Jameson turned to see Stephanie climbing out of a red compact car. She approached the grave, her own bunch of flowers in her hands.

The two sisters embraced.

Jameson moved to his truck, giving them privacy to mourn their sister. He leaned over the side of the truck bed, his hands folded, and thought about what it must be like to lose one of your siblings. He tried to imagine losing one of his brothers, visiting their grave every year, feeling the heavy weight of guilt that insisted there was something you could have done to prevent it. He could hardly bear to think about it, much less live it as these two girls were doing.

He murmured quietly to himself, "I can't imagine losing one of them. Don't know how I'd handle that."

The girls spent about a half an hour at the gravesite, and then they hugged each other goodbye. Ava walked back toward his truck, and her sister headed to her car.

Jameson opened the door for her, and she climbed in without a word. They were both quiet as they headed back across town. The rain picked up again, the temperature dropped.

Jameson reached across the space that separated

them and squeezed Ava's hand. She tried to give him a smile, but it didn't reach her eyes.

"I know what you need," he said, trying to cheer her up. A few minutes later, he pulled up to a small café.

She started to reach for her door handle, but he stopped her.

"Wait here. I'll be right back."

She nodded blankly at him as he exited the truck. Five minutes later he returned with a paper tray, two coffee cups nestled in it. He held one out to her. "Here, I got you a White Chocolate Mocha Espresso."

She stared at it. "Do you know how bad those are for you?"

He chuckled. "Well, sorry. They were all out of green slime smoothies."

"They're not slime."

"Right. Keep telling yourself that."

"They're very good for you."

He continued to hold the cup out to her until she finally took it with a secret smile that told him she really liked them. He paused, staring at her. "Oh, crap. You're gonna have me eating right, aren't you?"

She gave him a challenging look. "Yup."

"Shit."

"You just had no clue what you were in for when you took me on." She giggled.

He started the truck up, smiling. He'd gotten her laughing, and that was all that mattered.

CHAPTER TWENTY-FIVE

Jameson was up in his office Monday afternoon. He stood at the window, looking out over Main Street, his thumb moving over the screen of his cell phone. He put it to his ear. When the call was answered, he spoke. "Ryder? Jameson O'Rourke."

"O'Rourke. I was going to give you a call. You got any spots open up for me? I'll be back in town in two days."

"That all depends on you."

"Yeah? How's that?"

Jameson leaned a hand on the window frame, his eyes on the distant line of the horizon. "Had an issue the other night with one of your crew. Apparently it isn't the first, I'm finding out."

"What kind of issue?"

"Bald guy that was in with you? He's been harassing my girl. New one that works the front counter."

"Harassing? You want to elaborate on that."

"He broke into her place the other night. Was waiting inside when she came home. Jumped her. Luckily my brother showed up, and he took off."

"Did she involve the police?"

"Not yet. I thought you and I could work this out."

"Work it out how?"

"You want anymore work done in this shop, you'll make sure he stays away. She never lays eyes on him again, understand? Oh, and one other bit of information that may decide this for you. She's on the city council. Anything happens to her, are you really gonna want that kind of media attention?"

There was a long silence on the other end, and Jameson knew that Ryder didn't like being dictated to. And Jameson understood that, but he hoped the man would make the right decision and save them all further problems. He heard the man blow out a slow breath before the reply finally came.

"You've been a friend, O'Rourke. So, I'll do you that solid."

"Appreciated."

"Tell the lady she won't see him again."

"Thanks, Ryder."

"Reserve me that time."

"Done."

Jameson disconnected and slid his phone into his pocket, staring out his office window. He hoped that was the end of it. If not, it was going to kick up a shitstorm.

The phone on his desk rang. He glanced over to see the button lit up that indicated a call from Ava at the reception desk. He picked it up. "Yeah, babe?"

"There's a woman here to see you."

"I don't have an appointment scheduled now, do I?"

"No. She said her name is Courtney Kemp."

Well, I'll be damned. He smiled. "I'll be right down."

***

Ava hung up the phone and looked at the woman standing before her. She was older, perhaps fifty, but still beautiful. Her long dark hair was thick and silky without a hint of gray, and bespoke time in an expensive salon. She had on a pair of faded skinny jeans and heels, a peach colored silk blouse with tons of chains around her neck, and a snakeskin handbag over her arm that screamed money.

"He'll be right down, Ms. Kemp."

"Thank you."

The woman pushed a pair of designer sunglasses

up on her head, revealing dark brown eyes that reminded Ava of Penélope Cruz.

The sound of boot steps pounding down the stairs echoed through the shop. A moment later, Jameson came into view.

"Courtney, how're you doing, sweetheart?" He wrapped his arms around the woman, hugging her close.

Ava watched the two of them, studying every nuance. They broke apart.

"How have you been, love?" the woman asked Jameson, her hand on his chest.

"Things have been well. And you?"

"I've been in New York, darling. I was surprised to hear you had an art book being published."

He smiled at her, and it was in a way that made Ava feel there had to be history between these two—a long and possibly even an intimate history.

"I do."

"And then I come home and what do I see but posters up all over town that carry your picture, proclaiming you as headlining bachelor for the charity Gala next weekend."

Jameson's eyes shifted to Ava for a split second, and then he was guiding the woman toward the back.

JAMESON

"Come up to my office, and we'll catch up."

"I do hope you still keep a bottle of my favorite scotch."

Their voices trailed off as she heard Jameson assure her he did, and her soft laughter disappeared up the stairs.

Ava was surprised by the flare of jealousy that suddenly flamed to life inside her. She could think of nothing but that woman and Jameson and what she meant to him. The woman meant something; that was obvious. But why did it hurt so badly? Ava had only spent two nights with the man. Yes, they'd been phenomenal. But after all, until just recently, they hadn't even liked each other. Perhaps his feelings could flip back just as quickly.

Jameson had seemed happy to see the woman, and he'd wanted to spend time alone with her. What did that say? Ava wasn't sure. But it led her to believe that maybe she'd misjudged things, that maybe he didn't feel what she was beginning to feel for him. That was something she couldn't risk — making a fool of herself like that over him.

Her anger flared. A self defense mechanism of course, but that didn't make it any less genuine. She turned back to her desk, attempting to put it all aside and try to think of anything other than the fact that right now Jameson was upstairs alone with that beautiful woman.

About forty-five minutes later, Jameson escorted Ms. Kemp down the stairs and out the door. Ava could see through the plate glass window that he walked her to her car, which was parked right in front. They paused by the driver's door, talking and laughing. Then they hugged, and as they pulled apart, Ava saw them kiss. It was just a quick peck, but it was on the mouth.

He held the door while she climbed in. He leaned in, smiled, and said something, and then stepped back and shut her door. He stood watching her pull away.

When he came back in the shop, Ava pretended to be busy with the appointment calendar.

He paused next to her desk, leaning on his elbows with his arms folded. "You want to take a break?"

Without glancing at him, she replied, "Nope. I'm good."

She felt his eyes on her, but still she kept her gaze on the computer screen.

"You okay?" he asked.

"Yup. Fine."

She heard him move, and out of the corner of her

eye, she saw he was gone from the spot where he'd been standing. A split-second later, he was spinning her chair around, grasping her by the hand and pulling her up. He led her through the shop, down the hall, and into the private tattoo room.

Her eyes went wide as his hands went to her waist and plopped her up on the padded table. His palms pressed into the padded leather on either side of her knees. He stared at her.

"We have to stop meeting like this," she said sarcastically.

He tried to suppress a grin. "Don't be cute."

She shut up.

"You have questions. So ask them."

She frowned, not sure what he meant.

"Courtney Kemp. Ask me what you want to know. I'll tell you the truth."

Her chin came up. "All right, then, who is she to you?"

"Someone special. I'm sure you picked that up."

She nodded. "Yes. I did."

"She's a friend. She helped me when my parents died and everything went to shit. She was there for me. Loaned me money to set up here. I'll always be indebted to her."

"She was your... what? Benefactor?"

"I suppose you could call her that."

"Was that all there was between you?"

He studied her eyes, and then answered plainly, "No. For a short time we were lovers."

Ava swallowed. "Oh."

"That was years ago. We haven't been that to each other in a long fucking time."

She wouldn't look at him. "It's really none of my business."

"Isn't it?"

She glanced up at him then, frowning.

"We gonna talk about it?" His voice was firm.

"Talk about what?" she asked, even though she knew what he was referring to.

"The last two nights. Us. Or is it your plan to act like it didn't happen, like it didn't blow us both away."

"Oh, that."

"Yeah. *That*." The corner of his mouth pulled up.

"What is there to say?" she asked quietly, looking away.

He blew out a breath and cupped her cheek. "Hey, look at me." When she did, he continued. "I feel like all day we've both been walking on eggshells. That's not how I want it."

"That's not how I want it, either."

He studied her eyes. "I never expected this. It kind of caught me by surprise."

She gave him a tremulous smile. "Me, too."

"We can't just pretend this isn't happening."

She shook her head and then watched as his jaw clenched as if he was getting ready to admit something especially hard for him.

"Your perfume… It's in my clothes, in my bed. I can't get it out of my mind. How often do you think about what happened between us?"

She tried to look away. "All the time, but I feel like I pushed you into something you didn't want."

"It wasn't an accident, you and me."

"Wasn't it? If I hadn't been attacked, if you hadn't come rushing over to check on me…" She paused and shook her head. "Maybe circumstances pushed us into something that neither of us were ready for."

"Don't say that. Don't tell me you regret it." His soft plea brought her eyes back to his. "This has been a long time coming. We both know that. You've felt it. I know you have. This fire that burns whenever we get near each other."

"Yes," she admitted. "I've felt it."

He gave her that cocky grin he was so good at. "I'm

glad we got that cleared up."

She smiled back. "Me, too."

"Do you not see how everything has gotten better since we've stopped fighting it?"

Her eyes dropped shyly to her hands. "How could I not?"

"Ava, look at me." When she did, he searched her eyes. "Stuff happens in strange ways sometimes. Doesn't matter how we got here, just that we got here somehow."

She smiled, loving what he said and how he made her face head-on what was happening between them.

"You need a little more persuading?" Without waiting for her answer, his mouth came down on hers, and once again he showed her just how good they were together.

When they finally broke apart, she couldn't help the radiant smile on her face as she looked up at how happy he seemed. It was good to see him happy. And she liked that it was her who made him feel that way.

"I love seeing you smile. I need this, Ava." He gave her a quick peck and then pulled back. "I have to make a trip to Denver tomorrow. I want you with me."

Her brows drew together. "Denver? For what?"

"I've got this coffee table book coming out with

photos of some of my work. The book Courtney was referring to. The publishers arranged a signing for me."

"What do you need me for?"

"I need a P.A."

"What's a P.A.?"

"Personal assistant."

She shook her head, grinning. "No you don't."

He grinned back, caught in the lie. "Would you come if I just told you I want you with me?"

"Because of that guy?"

"I won't lie. That's part of it. But I also want you to come with me."

She looked down. "Jameson—"

"It's just two nights."

"I don't know."

"I think it'll be good for us. Get away from everything. Try and figure out what this is between us."

She searched his eyes, thinking maybe he was right; maybe they did need some time to figure things out. She knew she certainly did. Finally, she nodded. "All right."

CHAPTER TWENTY-SIX

Ava sat in the passenger side of Jameson's big black pickup truck. They were a little over two hours into the four-hour trip to Denver, just passing the town of Vail. On her right, Ava could see the slopes and trails, their swatches of summer green grass cutting swathes across the wooded mountains. They looked odd without the snow and colorfully dressed skiers moving down them.

Jameson turned up the stereo. "This is my favorite song that Rory's band does."

She smiled, listening to the music. "They're quite good aren't they?"

"Yes, they are."

"That scares you, doesn't it?"

His eyes swung to her for a moment, a frown on his face, before he returned his attention to the road. "Why do you say that?"

"What if they make it big? That's bound to break up that tight family unit you've worked so hard to hold onto."

She could tell her words hit home. He ran a hand over his jaw. "My focus has always been to keep this family together, that's true."

"You're very defensive to anything that threatens it."

"I've had to be."

"In the past, that was probably true."

"Probably?"

She ignored his comment. "Take for example that girl from Utah, the one you ran off."

"What about her? She was bad news. Rory doesn't need that in his life."

"Maybe, maybe not, but it was his decision to make. He's a grown man. They all are. With dreams and aspirations of their own. Maybe they'll want something other than the tattoo shop someday. You can't rule them with an iron fist forever."

"Is that what you think I do?"

"Don't you?"

He huffed out a breath. "I'll always worry about the women they date. That probably won't ever change. And I know I need it to be my way or the highway, I admit it. I know that may drive Liam away."

"He has a lot of ideas about the shop, doesn't he?"

"He does." His eyes flicked to her. "Your little

presentation didn't help. Talking about the new systems and all they could do for us—when you got to the part about being able to connect between several locations, several shops, I think I literally saw the light bulb go on above Liam's head."

"He'd like his own shop?"

"He'd like to run things his own way, different from the way I do."

"How so?"

"He's edgier. I don't know how to explain it. I just know his shop would look nothing like the one we have now."

"Yours looks more like an art gallery."

"Exactly. His would look much more old-school, grittier, darker. And there's absolutely a market for that."

"What if he did break off and opened a second location of Brothers Ink?"

"I honestly don't know. I don't even want to think about it."

"What about Max? Is tattooing his first love?"

"Max enjoys working at the shop; I think he's happy. But he does spend a lot of time at the gym. He's developed quite a fascination with boxing and mixed martial arts."

"And you're worried that may pull him away?"

"Maybe."

"The very thing you fear most is coming about."

"I realize that. I realize I can't keep the family together forever. My brothers have their own lives to lead. I can't be the one to hold them back. I don't want to be that man." He looked over at her, and she could see the emotion in his eyes.

"Jameson, you have to let the tight grip go, or you're going to lose the very thing you're trying to hold onto. Your brothers are grown. They can make their own decisions and choices."

He huffed out another laugh. "Telling me how to run my life?"

She smiled at him. "Just offering a little observation."

"Okay, how about we turn the tables, and I tell you what I've observed? Think you can handle that, lady?"

She turned away.

"What? You can dish it out, but you can't take it?"

She turned back to him and lifted her chin. "Okay, fine. Fire away."

His eyes shifted to the highway, one hand on the wheel, the other brushing over his mouth. She studied him closely, and it seemed like he was considering his words carefully before he spoke.

"We're both the oldest. I know what that's like. I know what it's like to feel responsible for the others. But Ava, you are not responsible for what happened to your sister. You have to let go of the guilt. I know you loved her very much, but, sweetheart, you have to start living for yourself. You can't live your life making it just about the charity and Lily's memory."

He paused to stare over at her, but she remained mute. His words hit so close to home. She felt her throat close up. She made a soft protest. "I don't, I—"

"You do. You're consumed by it."

She got quiet.

"What about what *you* want? Doesn't that ever figure in?" he asked softly.

"It's hard to let go of the guilt. I've carried it for so long."

"It's not your fault. She wouldn't want this for you."

She looked down, her thumbnail scratching at the label on her water bottle.

"You know that, Ava. You have to know that."

"I understand that no matter what I do, I'll never bring Lily back. But—"

"Don't you ever live? Live just for you?"

"Maybe I don't ride motorcycles, or mountain bikes, or play a guitar, or...or... fight MMA, but that doesn't mean I don't live."

"Sweetheart, I didn't mean—"

"Yes, you did. You think I have a boring life, that I have no rebellious spirit, but—"

"Ava, the woman who let me give her a piercing and a tattoo has plenty of spirit. That's what I'm trying to say. That's the woman I want to see you let shine. Stop burying it under all this duty and responsibility and guilt. And just live, Ava. Free and easy and fun-loving, like I know you can."

"Can we please stop talking about this?"

"You started it."

She looked over at him then and found him grinning. She rolled her eyes. "You sound like a six-year-old."

He stuck his tongue out at her, and she burst out laughing. Then he reached over and pulled her to him.

"C'mere."

When her head leaned in, he kissed the top of it and ruffled his hand through her hair. "You hungry, babe?"

She smiled. "I'm starved."

"Good, 'cause I'm through with this therapy

session we have goin' on. How 'bout we get a burger and a beer?"

"Sounds like a plan."

***

They arrived in Denver a couple of hours later. Jameson pulled the truck into a parking garage of a high-rise condominium in the middle of downtown. They grabbed their overnight bags and took an elevator to the lobby. He moved to the reception desk and spoke with the woman behind it. He was given a key, and they headed to the elevator. Getting in, he pushed the button for one of the upper floors.

"You have a condo here?"

"Renting it for a couple nights. It's on the market, though, and the realtor is pushing for a sale."

"You're thinking of buying a place here in Denver? Why?"

He shrugged. "Rory plays in Denver quite a bit. And all this talk of opening a second location has got me thinking. I had a lot of pressure to move to L.A. when I was doing the TV show. Maybe Denver could be the compromise."

She gave him a knowing smile. "Hmm. Jameson O'Rourke, I didn't think you knew the meaning of the word."

He backed her into the wall of the elevator. "Babe, feels like the only thing I've done since I met you is one compromise after another."

"What we seem to always end up with are deals and bets. And you do seem to negotiate those quite well for yourself."

He grinned. "Isn't that what compromises are made of? Negotiations?"

"Somehow those compromises always seem to work in your favor, though, don't they?"

"Maybe I just negotiate better than you," he teased, nuzzling her neck.

The elevator stopped, and the doors slid open. Jameson led her down the hall, stopped in front of one of the doors and inserted the key. When it swung open and she walked in, the first thing she noticed was the floor-to-ceiling expanse of windows that surrounded the corner unit on two sides.

The furnishings were all modern with sleek lines and monochromatic grays and blacks against a polished travertine cream floor. The paintings on the wall were a combination of modern and post-modern art.

She moved to the window to take in the view of the city and mountains beyond. "Oh, Jameson. Look at that view."

He came to stand a few feet behind her. She spun around, taking in the room. "It's beautiful. Are you really thinking of buying this place?"

He shrugged. "Considering it."

She cocked her head. "When did you meet with a realtor here?"

"Right before I stormed into your office. I'd been in Denver. When I got back in town, the first thing I saw was that flyer of yours up all over the place."

"Oh." She sucked her lips in. "So, you were thinking of another location even before you met me?"

"At the time I was thinking more along the lines of a place for Rory to crash when he was in town."

She gave him a doubting expression. "You'd let the band crash here? They'd trash the place."

He grinned. "Yeah. Maybe you're right."

She glanced around again. "You can afford this?"

"Well, that's what happens when you scrimp and save and don't blow your money on new computer systems," he teased with a grin.

"Yeah, sure."

"Okay, that and a shitload of TV money."

"Now that, I believe."

"And a book deal."

"Right. The reason we're here."

"The reason we're here. Yes, ma'am." He glanced at his watch. "Speaking of which, I've got a meeting with some people in about an hour. You gonna be good to hang here for a while?"

"Of course."

He took her face in his hands and tilted it up. His mouth was just inches away from hers as he said, "I'm glad you came."

"Me, too," she breathed.

He pressed a barely-there kiss to her lips. "I'll show you how much when I get back."

She smiled. "I'll hold you to that."

He kissed her again and left.

***

Ava lay in the dark, draped across Jameson's slowly rising and falling chest. He had passed out after their second round of sex that night. Now Ava stared across him and out the big windows of the master bedroom at the city lights beyond the sheer curtains and thought about how she felt about this man who had barreled into her life with all the finesse of a freight train.

He'd returned from his meeting with bags of Thai food, and they'd curled up on the couch with it. She felt so comfortable with him. They'd laughed and told stories from their childhoods and growing up. Chatting with a man had never felt so natural before. It was like she could finally relax and let her guard down. Now that they'd stopped fighting and antagonizing, they both realized just how much they truly enjoyed each other's company.

Her eyes dropped to the ink that covered his chest, and she couldn't stop her hand from reaching out, her fingers tracing along the colorful lines. She followed along from his breastbone, over his ribs and down. She got to his hipbone before his hand came up and closed over hers, stilling her motion.

"You ready for another go 'round, babe?" His other palm slid over her ass cheek and squeezed.

"Just admiring your ink."

"You like my ink? I figured you for a woman who'd hate men with tattoos."

"On you, they look good."

His palm rubbed over her ass cheek again and then roved up over the soft skin of her back. "I'd love to put some more on you."

She lifted her head to look up at him with a grin. "You would?"

He cracked an eye open. "Yes, ma'am."

"What would you put?"

"I love the way the design I put on your hip peeks around at me when I fuck you from behind. I'd like to do something on the other side as well. And maybe something on your back."

"What about my breasts?" she asked in a teasing voice.

He grinned as he pulled her up so his eyes could take them in as if he were considering. "Mmm. Nope. I'd leave them alone. Why mess with perfection?"

That had her lowering her head to catch his mouth in a kiss. Two seconds later he was rolling, taking her down to the mattress. He pinned her hands to the bed.

She smiled up at him. "Perfection, huh?"

His eyes ran over her breasts again. "Absolutely." Then he lowered his head and showed her just how much he liked them.

CHAPTER TWENTY-SEVEN

Ava stood watching as Jameson sat at a table in the back of the huge bookstore. There was a line of people that snaked through the store and out the doors. Almost everyone in the line was inked, but Ava noticed a lot of young women who were not, but were most definitely infatuated with Jameson's good looks and bad-boy appearance. Men, women, teens… they all bought his book by the pallets full.

He took time with each fan, personalizing their copy, smiling and laughing with them, and even posing for pictures. Ava stayed nearby, in the background a bit, ready to keep him supplied with bottles of water, fresh pens, or anything else he might need. She noticed he glanced at her often, making sure she was still by his side. When the publicists and store managers tried to shuffle her to the background, Jameson quickly set them straight.

It didn't take long for one of the women who — Ava

discovered—was with the production company for the reality show he'd done, to find her. Apparently the woman had noticed the importance with which Jameson labeled her.

She stuck her hand out, credentials around her neck swinging. "I'm Becca Thompson. DRH Productions. How do you do?"

Ava shook her hand. "Ava Hightower. Pleased to meet you."

"And how do you know Mr. O'Rourke?" the woman asked her.

"I own a staffing company in Grand Junction, and I'm on the city council. Jameson and I are...friends."

The woman nodded, not buying that description of their relationship for a moment. "So, you're both business owners, huh?"

"Yes."

"Do you have any pull with him?"

"Pull?"

"We're trying to lock up negotiations for a second season of *Inked Up*. The network is pushing hard for an L.A. based shoot. We're trying to get the loose ends wrapped up, which is why they sent me down here for his book release."

"A second season? I thought the show was

cancelled."

"Cancelled? Are you kidding? That show was huge. We've been begging him to commit to a second season." Her phone rang, and she glanced down at it. "I'm sorry, I really have to take this. But it was lovely meeting you, Ava, dear. And anything you can do to push Jamie along, we'd love to get this locked down while he's here in Denver."

Ava frowned at the woman and nodded. It really didn't matter, though; Ms. Thompson was already pushing through the crowd to find a quieter spot to take her call.

Ava's eyes swung back to Jameson who was admiring the ink on a fan's arm. Why had he let everyone think the show had been cancelled? Was he really thinking of going to L.A.? Why hadn't he said anything? And why did the thought of him leaving town upset her so? She felt suddenly like her dog had just died, and she didn't even have a dog.

***

After the signing, Ms. Thompson offered to take them both out to dinner, but Jameson put her off, instead agreeing to meet with her in the morning. She wasn't happy, but she was still sucking up in order to leave Denver with what she came for. So she agreed.

That night, Jameson took Ava to a nice restaurant two blocks from the condo. He ordered them a bottle of wine. When it was brought and poured, he raised his glass to toast.

"Are we celebrating something?" Ava asked.

"To a very successful trip and to the company of a beautiful woman."

They clinked glasses.

"You certainly did well today. I think they said you sold out two pallets."

He flexed his hand. "It's sore as hell from all that signing. It kept cramping up on me."

"Better be careful. That's the hand you tattoo with." She smiled at him.

He chuckled and rolled his eyes as he lifted the wine glass to his mouth. "Right. That's the bread and butter, after all, isn't it?"

"You know as much demand as there is for all things 'Jameson O'Rourke', you should start a line of t-shirts with some of your art on them or your name or the shop's name. Judging from today, they'd sell out. I bet all those people today would have bought one. They'd fly off the shelves."

A grin pulled at the corner of his mouth. "I like the way you think, Ava."

"Why stop there? You can sell posters and prints of your art."

"You're brilliant." He winked at her. "Maybe I should put you in charge of publicity and marketing."

At the mention of publicity, she looked down, twirling the stem of her wine glass on the white tablecloth. Thoughts of the *Inked Up* offer, as well as all the pressure they were putting on him to relocate to L.A., filled her head. But that was his decision, and she didn't really want to let on that she knew anything about it. He'd have his meeting with Ms. Becca Thompson in the morning. He'd make his decision, perhaps he already had. Would he accept? It was a lot to pass up, after all. The money, the fame, the book deals… How did one say no to all that? And for what? To stay in Grand Junction? What was keeping him there? A family home? His brothers? Love? No, she couldn't even think that way. She had no hold on him. If he decided to leave, she'd miss him, but she would try to be happy for him. And perhaps if it was going to happen, it would be best it happened now before she got in too deep, before she got really attached, before she actually fell for the man and had her heart broken when he left town. She looked up, catching his eyes on her.

"What are you thinking about, beautiful?"

She shook her head, not about to admit all that to him, but staring into his blue eyes, she couldn't help wondering if it was already too late. If perhaps, she'd already fallen hopelessly in love with the complicated man who sat across from her.

***

After they finished dinner they walked hand-in-hand down the two blocks to the condo. He kept glancing over at her. They'd say nothing—just exchange smiles. The day had been warm, but now a cool breeze blew in from the front range of the mountains.

When they got back to the condo, he walked her into the bedroom. He set his phone and keys down on the nightstand, and she moved to the windows, her hand parting the sheers to take in the gorgeous view. She heard his clothing rustling and knew he was undressing. He came up behind her, sliding his hands around her waist. She felt him press kisses along her neck.

"You can look at the view tomorrow, beautiful."

He turned her and gathered her hands in his, and then, his eyes burning into hers, he lifted her arms and pinned them to the glass.

He leaned in and brushed his lips across hers—a barely-there touch, that had her straining for more, but he pulled back. The look in his eyes told her he was taking control. He moved both her wrists, trapping them in one big hand.

His free hand moved to her waist, flicking open the fastening of her pants. Never losing her gaze, he slid his hand inside her panties, his fingers delving to find her wet.

She whimpered and watched the flare of heat in his eyes.

He leaned close, whispering, "That sound, *goddamn*, it's pushing me over the edge."

"Jameson," she whispered in a trembling voice as he rolled his fingers over her. His eyes stayed locked with hers as he continued the circular motion until her mouth parted and her breath began to come in short pants.

"You like when I touch you. Don't you, Ava?"

She nodded, feeling incapable of words, but that wasn't good enough for him. Pushing, always pushing her for more.

"Say it, baby. Say it."

"Yes. I like when you touch me. I love it."

His mouth closed over hers again as he continued

stroking until he had her hovering on the edge of orgasm.

"Ask for it."

"Please."

"Say it."

"Let me come."

He increased the strokes to long deep swipes, and soon she climaxed as he smothered her moans with his mouth. She melted against the sheer covered glass, and his strong arms held her up. He held her until her breathing evened out, and then slowly, piece by piece, he undressed her, standing right where she was with nothing but sheer curtains between her and the outside world. When she was naked, his hand locked around her wrist.

He pulled her toward the bed, sat, and drew her to stand between his legs. Just being trapped between his thighs aroused her all over again. The look in his eyes fanned her desire, and she wanted nothing more than to please him.

She dropped to her knees, her hands on his thighs, and looked up at him. His eyes flared, and he cupped her face, his hands sliding into her hair.

Her fingers skated along his skin and then closed over his hardened length. She slid her fist down and back up, barely brushing his flesh.

"Harder," he instructed. She did as he asked, stroking up and down, watching the expression on his face as she touched him. He breathed out through his nose, eyes narrowing, jaw clenching. His hand closed over hers, showing her exactly the tempo he liked and how hard. He bit his lip, his eyes fixed on her as his breathing accelerated with her pace.

Soon, it wasn't enough. His brows lowered, and his jaw tightened as he clenched his teeth and growled, "I want that pretty mouth on me."

She locked her eyes with his as she stroked his length, then leaned in slowly and took him into her mouth. She felt him shudder as she sank down, and his hips lifted off the bed.

He threaded both hands into her hair, gripping handfuls and tugging firmly. "You don't know how often I've thought about this—wrapping your hair around my fist and pulling you down onto me."

He didn't force or push her onto him, he just gathered her hair in his fists, and she loved the feel of his hands in her hair, controlling, allowing, coaxing.

She took him deep again and again, loving the way she could feel the tremors through his thighs and the way his fist in her hair tightened involuntarily as he began to thrust up into her mouth.

"Fuck, baby. Love your mouth."

Before long he was nearing his climax. "I want inside you."

She moaned, and the next thing Ava new, she was yanked up and tossed onto the bed. His hard muscled body climbed over her, and he stared down into her eyes with a sexual heat that ratcheted up her arousal to off-the-charts heights.

Her breathing, already panting, was even harder with his body braced atop hers and that intense stare burning into her. She felt as if he could see everything; she was totally exposed, and maybe that was what she needed—him to push her to show him everything, to hold nothing back.

He rested his weight on one forearm, freeing his other hand to stroke and caress her. She stroked her hand down his arm, but he caught it, bringing it up over her head and locking it tight with his other hand on her wrist.

"Lie still," he ordered.

She did, blowing out a slow breath. That freed him to touch her at his leisure.

He ran his fingers over her body—light feathery touches that tickled and made her writhe. Then his palm smoothed flat and slid up her belly to her breast, closing tightly around it.

She moaned.

"You like a firm touch, don't you, baby?"

She nodded. "Yes."

He pinched her nipple, squeezing and rolling the tip until her back arched off the bed. "I'm gonna make you want me as much as you just made me want you."

He replaced his fingers with his mouth, sucking with deep, drawing pulls that had her writhing and twisting and arching, begging with her body for more. He didn't let up until a frustrated groan sounded in her throat.

Tearing his mouth away, he lifted his head a fraction of an inch, hovering over her wet nipple as he stared up at her, panting hard. Her head was lifted off the bed, although he still held her wrist pinned above. Her eyes held his as her chest rose and fell.

"Tell me what you want, sweetheart," he ordered.

Her hips rose off the bed, rubbing against him, and he swiveled his head, lifting his weight and watching his fingers slide into her. She moved against his touch in a rhythmic glide. "That's it, baby. Don't be afraid to take what you want." His head turned back to watch the expression on her face as he stroked her. His eyes dilated as he took in the pure arousal written in everything from the way her mouth dropped open to the way her head fell back, driving the crown of her head into the pillow. "That's it. Take what you need, baby doll."

He watched every reaction as he brought her to the edge and over, her body jerking with her orgasm. In a flash, he moved up over her, kissing her deep, capturing her moans in his mouth. And then just as quickly, he was moving back and flipping her to her stomach. His knees spread her thighs wide with a forceful movement. With one hand locked tight on her hip and the other guiding him to her entrance, he slammed home. Pulling her against him, he pounded into her over and over until he, too, found his climax.

***

Ava lay in Jameson's arms, facing the windows and the view of the city lights. He was pressed against her back, his arms around her. She ran her hand over his strong forearm and thought about everything. She had a feeling he was going to take the offer Becca Thompson planned to extend to him tomorrow morning. Why shouldn't he?

She didn't want to be the reason he refused. He had a big future ahead of him, and she didn't want to be the one to hold him back. So, she would make it easy for him. She'd tell him this was fun, but it was all just part of the deal, all with the end goal in mind—her Gala, her charity.

Which brought her thoughts full circle. *Lily.* Jameson was right. She had to let go of the guilt; she had to let go of Lily. Oh, she'd always be in her heart, but Ava had to start living for herself. She would always be grateful to him for making her face it and for pushing her to explore a side of herself she hadn't known existed.

The Gala was this weekend. She would focus on that, and then somehow, she would let Jameson walk out of her life.

CHAPTER TWENTY-EIGHT

Ava woke up and stretched out an arm, finding the bed next to her empty. Then she swiveled her head toward the door. Jameson stood in the doorway, shirtless, with a pair of trousers on. His hands were in his hip pockets as he leaned against the doorframe. His eyes were hooded, still sleepy, his hair a sexy mess.

Her gaze moved over the expanse of exposed skin on display. It made her want to slide her hands over every inch. Now that she'd experienced all that was Jameson, and knew what she'd been missing, she felt like she would never get enough. But she also knew she was probably going to have to let him go.

Not yet… Not until their trip was over.

"Keep looking at me like that, Ava and I'll miss my meeting, and you won't be able to walk tomorrow," he warned.

God, if he only knew how much she selfishly wanted him to miss that meeting. But she would never purposely sabotage him like that. Still, a little teasing might be fun. She pushed the sheet aside, moving to her knees, with her feet tucked under her ass. Their eyes met and held.

A moment later, he was pushing his shoulder from the frame and stalking toward her. His hands came out of his pockets, and he grabbed her face, pulling her up as his mouth closed over hers. She pressed her breasts to his bare belly, arching against him. "Come back to bed, baby."

He bit her lip and then stared down at her face. She watched his eyes move lower to take in her breasts, the tips just barely touching his skin. It drove her crazy. He grinned, knowing it.

"You gonna be naked when I get back?"

"Is that what you want?" she asked, wondering where this new wanton hussy had come from.

"While I'm sitting through that boring meeting, I want to imagine you lying here naked, waiting for me."

"Okay," she agreed breathlessly.

"Will you do something for me, if I ask?"

She nodded, her head still tight in his grasp as she stared up at him.

"Text me something dirty while I'm there." She giggled out a tinkling laugh and he grinned, reminding her again where he wanted her. "Right here, naked."

She nodded.

He pulled her head close for a kiss and then released her, grabbed a shirt and tie, and sauntered from the room.

***

A half hour later, Ava did as he'd asked.

I'm sliding my fingers through my wetness, remembering the way you felt inside me.

She didn't have to wait long for the reply.

> *You have no idea how badly I want to fuck you right now.*

She giggled.

You've turned me into such a dirty slut.

> *I don't like that word, Ava. I may have to spank you when I get back.*

Oh my. Now I really am wet.

> *Counting the minutes until I can get my hands on you again, babe.*

***

Ava stood in the living room in front of the wall of windows, staring out over the Front Range lit up in vibrant colors by the afternoon sun. Jameson was down turning in the key.

When he had returned from his meeting, he'd found her waiting naked for him, just like she'd promised. He'd stood in the doorway, yanking his tie free, his eyes roving over her. She'd lain there, staring at him, sliding one foot across the sheet, enticing him to come to her. He'd dropped his head, looking at her from under his brow, and she'd bit her lip, the corners of her mouth pulling up. And then he'd smiled back at her with that sexy as hell grin.

They'd spent two more glorious hours rolling around the sheets. But now, it was time to head back to Grand Junction; time for their glorious little interlude to end. Most upsetting of all, the time had come for her to let him go. She knew she had to be strong. It was what was best for him, and she'd never stand in his way.

She turned at the sound of the door opening to see Jameson walk in.

"Hey, sweetheart. Sorry it took so long. You ready to go?"

She pasted a bright smile on her face. "All packed. You never told me how your meeting went?"

"It went very well. All wrapped up. But I don't want to talk business. Are you hungry?"

She knew right then that he'd accepted Ms. Thompson's offer. Why else wouldn't he want to talk about it? He just didn't want to tell her he would be leaving town. She gathered up her purse. "Starved. Can we hit a donut shop? I'd love a coffee and donut."

He nodded. "Absolutely. Let me just grab our bags."

***

Twenty minutes later, they were in the truck, coffee and donuts in hand, and heading down the highway. Jameson popped the last of his into his mouth and crumbled up the wax paper, stuffing it back in the paper bag.

Ava did the same and sipped her coffee.

He glanced over at her. "You okay? You're so quiet."

"Just ready to get back. I have a lot of preparation to get ready for the Gala Saturday night."

"Right. Of course."

"I hope you don't mind if I don't come into the shop the next two days. I mean our deal is coming to an end."

His brows drew together, and he studied her strangely. "Yeah, of course. You need time to get ready for the event. I understand."

"Good. It's been fun learning the tattoo business, but now its time to get back to the real world. I bet there's a ton of work piled up at my office."

He stared out the windshield. Things had been fine between them last night and this morning. Hell, *better* than fine. Now things had seemed to chill. She was suddenly acting as if none of it meant anything to her.

"I'll be sure to send over a tux for you to wear," she added, looking out the passenger window.

"That won't be necessary," he snapped.

She turned to look at him, frowning. "What do you mean?"

"I have a suit I can wear. I do have the ability to clean up. I can dress myself."

"I didn't mean…"

"I know what you meant."

"It's just that it's black tie and…"

"I highly doubt the women coming because of me, expect me in a tux. Hell, they'll probably want to see the ink. Maybe I should do this gig shirtless." Now he was being a jerk, he knew, but he couldn't stop himself.

He stared out the windshield. He wasn't gonna lie, at least not to himself. Her callous attitude hurt and the way she just trivialized what they'd shared the last week, like it meant nothing to her but a means to an end, pissed him off.

The trip back was filled with tension. They both barely said a word after that and hardly looked at each other. When he finally hit the city limits, he glanced over at her. "You don't have to be afraid of that guy who broke into your home. I spoke with Ryder. He'll make sure you never lay eyes on him again."

She stared over at him, wide-eyed. "You talked to him about what happened?"

"Yeah. Called him Monday."

"I didn't know. You never said."

"Well, I did."

"Thank you."

"No problem."

She looked down at her hands a moment. "Do you think... do you think he'll stay away?"

"Absolutely. Ryder runs that crew with an iron fist. You won't have to worry about him anymore."

"Okay."

He glanced over at her. "You can come home with me, or I can take you to your place. Your choice."

She met his eyes and then looked away. "I really should get back, I've so much to do with the Gala and all."

"Sure. Whatever you want," he said coldly.

Five minutes later, he pulled the truck to the curb in front of her house. Getting out, he came around and pulled her bag out of the back and carried it to her door. "I know I said you'd be safe, but I can come in and make sure no one's inside if it'll make you feel better," he offered.

She nodded. "Thank you."

He carried her bag and briefly checked around inside. Satisfied, he turned to leave, pausing in the doorway. His eyes hit her, and he couldn't stop himself from asking, "Ava, is everything okay? Did I do something or—?"

She shook her head. "No, Jameson, I'm just tired."

He hated that things had changed between them somewhere on the trip. And it drove him crazy that he didn't know why. But his pride kept him from making a fool out of himself if he'd misread the situation, and she didn't return the feelings he'd been starting to develop for her. He nodded. "Okay, then. I guess I'll see you Saturday night."

"Yes. Saturday. If you could be there a half hour

before the event starts, that would be great."

"Yeah. No problem. Take care." He turned and left without a kiss, without even a touch. If what they had was over, he'd better accept it and be done with it.

CHAPTER TWENTY-NINE

The night of the Gala, Ava was backstage. The hall was filled with people, all in black tie attire. Bars were set up in several locations. Hors d'oeuvres were being passed on silver trays by wait staff. A DJ played music, and some of the crowd were dancing.

The bachelor auction was about to begin. Ava was lining the men up. A popular local TV newswoman would play auctioneer, introduce the men, and get the crowd going. There were twenty men scheduled. Each would walk down the little runway as the host spoke about them and the DJ played upbeat music.

It was just about time for the auctioneer to call the hall to attention. The buzz in the crowd was growing as the lights dimmed and the music changed.

Ava spotted Jameson at the end of the lineup. He had his brothers all with him, each in a well-dressed suit. She moved to greet them.

"Hi, guys. Thanks for coming."

"Ava, darlin'." Max pulled her in for a hug, then moved back, his eyes sweeping down over the black strapless gown she wore. "Don't you look gorgeous."

Next was Liam's turn. "Come here, beautiful."

Then Rory hugged her. "Hey, sweetheart."

Lastly stood Jameson. His eyes moved over her. "Ava."

"Jameson." She nodded. Why did things have to be so uncomfortable and awkward now? Her eyes moved over his black suit, stark white shirt, and gray tie. She smiled. "You clean up well."

The corner of his mouth pulled up in half a grin. "Want to give the ladies their money's worth, right?"

She broke her gaze from his to take in all of them. "So am I to understand Max is also going to participate?"

"They all are," Jameson replied and handed her some papers. "Here, I had them fill out copies of the form you sent me the other day."

Ava had given Jameson a copy of the information sheet she'd asked each bachelor to complete for the auction. It contained fun facts about each man, like his favorite foods, sports or activities he participated in, etcetera. It was so the auctioneer could have something to work with when she made commentary as each bachelor walked the runway.

She accepted the forms. "Really? That's wonderful. If you'll excuse me, I'll go inform our host we've got some additions." She made a hasty retreat, glad to have an excuse to walk away. It had been terribly awkward with Jameson, and it hurt so much to pretend like what they'd shared hadn't meant anything. But even as she made her exit, she felt Jameson's eyes upon her, watching her run away like the scared little coward he must think she was. If only he knew how much courage it took to walk away from a life with him.

***

A few minutes later, the auction began.

"Good evening ladies and gentlemen," the auctioneer said. "We have quite a crowd here tonight. The fun is just beginning, I promise you. I hope you've all had time to mingle with tonight's bachelors and got to drop your answers in the boxes to the trivia questions about each of them. We'll be pulling winners to each for some special prizes we'll be giving away at the end of the evening. Right now though, we'd like to get the auction started. So, get out your checkbooks, ladies, and please join us as we raise lots of money for this very worthwhile cause."

From backstage, Ava watched the proceedings. She

couldn't help but observe the O'Rourke brothers at the back of the pack as Jameson flagged over a waiter and whispered something to him. A few moments later, he returned with a tray of four shots. The men lifted them up in the air and then downed them.

She turned her attention back to the proceedings.

As each bachelor walked, the crowd grew more excited. The auctioneer was doing a great job rousing the crowd with her fun commentary. The bachelors were all getting into it, playing along with enthusiasm, some dancing down the runway. So far the bids had stayed in the mid and upper hundreds. Ava hoped they would go up as each bachelor came out.

"Ladies, things are about to get hot in here tonight. I'd like you to meet Clint Jackson, a Grand Junction fire fighter. Clint enjoys putting out fires, saving lives and saving damsels in distress. How much am I bid?"

The women were soon bidding back and forth, the price climbing higher.

He took off his jacket and did a handstand and then a backflip.

"And he's flexible, ladies."

They all hooted and screamed.

"I've got $575 in the back, can we get $600? Going once, twice, sold for $600 dollars to the lady in gold."

Soon it was down to the four men from Brothers Ink. Rory was up first. With his long hair and rock-star looks, he had the crowd hooting and whistling as he came out on stage. The auctioneer introduced him.

"Next up we have Rory O'Rourke. Some of you may know him from his work as a tattoo artist at Brothers Ink and appearing with those brothers on the hit show *Inked Up*," she paused for the roar in applause and whistles. "And some of you may know him as the lead guitarist and front man from the band Convicted Chrome." There were even louder cheers.

Rory walked down the runway, he paused at the end, turning and sliding his hands in his pockets. The silver bracelets he wore flashed in the spotlights. Calvin Klein's top models had nothing on him as he scanned the crowd, that cute little pirate smile making each woman swoon.

"How much am I bid for a date with this gorgeous man, ladies?"

Bids were shouted back and forth and soon climbed to the thousand mark. Ava stood just on the edge of the curtain, watching, open-mouthed as the bids soon surpassed the two thousand mark.

Rory ended up going to a beautiful brunette that Ava knew was an assistant district attorney for $3000.

He exited the stage down a set of steps to greet the woman. It was left up to the bachelor and winning bidder to work out the details of the date.

Up next was Liam. As he strode out onto the stage, the mood in the hall was raucous. The auctioneer began to describe him, and to a striptease beat, Liam took his jacket off, tossing it into the crowd to the screams of the women. Then he undid his tie, leaving it hanging around his neck while he slowly unbuttoned his shirt, pulling the tails free. As the screams and bids went higher, he slowly drew his tie off and twirled it, then flicked it like a whip.

"Things are getting racy now," the auctioneer laughed into the microphone. "I think he's looking for a bad girl, ladies, one who needs some discipline."

That got all the women screaming.

In the end, Liam ended up going for $2500.

Next up was Max. He soon was yanking his tie off and tossing his jacket aside to reveal he'd torn the sleeves off his dress shirt. When the women got a look at his huge biceps, covered in tribal tattoos, they went crazy. He posed and flexed. The crowd of women began to scream for the shirt to come off. He didn't disappoint, shimmying it off after a few teasing moves to reveal rock hard abs. The bidding finally topped off

JAMESON

at $2800.

As the women all cheered him on as he came down the steps to the winning bidder, the auctioneer called their attention to the next bachelor.

"And now, ladies, the man you've all been waiting for, the man of the hour, the star of the show, *Inked Up*... the King of Ink himself, Jameson O'Rourke!"

There was a roar, unlike anything the hall had heard up until that point. Jameson strolled out, his hands in his pockets. His eyes moved over the crowd and he smiled that sexy little smile Ava knew he was capable of, but had only seen once or twice. The music changed to a driving rock beat, all comedy aside, as he strolled down the runway.

"He likes mountain biking, art of any kind, and Thai food. He rides a Harley and he's got several piercings. I leave that to your imagination, girls." There were some high-pitched screams. "And ladies, he's got an artist's touch I'm sure you could persuade him to put to good use."

There were more screams and whistles.

Jameson looked back at the auctioneer. "I'll throw a free tattoo into the date." Then he turned back to the audience, his eyes moving slowly over the crowd as he gave them his best wolf's smile. "If any of you ladies are wild enough."

That threw the crowd into a frenzy and bidding intensified to a furious pace. They were approaching $5000 when a voice in the crowd shouted, "Ten thousand!"

From her position behind the curtain, Ava couldn't see the area from which the bid had come. But she saw Jameson's eyes as he zeroed in on the bidder, and the big grin that formed on his face.

The auctioneer yelled out, "Going once, going twice," then slammed the gavel down. "Sold, for ten thousand dollars to the lady in red."

Ava stepped around the curtain and moved to the podium. As the organizer and host of the event, she would announce the final amount they'd raised this evening. One of the assistants stepped forward to hand her the tally he'd been running, adding in all the auction amounts.

Ava greeted the auctioneer, who shook her hand and stepped away from the microphone. Ava leaned to it. "Thank you so much, Tanya. Let's have a round of applause for tonight's auctioneer. From channel 7, KLRS news anchor…Tanya Davis."

There was more applause.

"And how about a round of applause for our

bachelors?" she added. As another roar went up, Ava's eyes found Jameson. He was standing next to a woman in a red evening gown. It was then Ava realized it was Courtney Kemp, the woman who'd come to see him at the shop. Jameson stared back at her and something about the way he looked at her was almost challenging, like he dared her to do something.

Seeing him with Courtney Kemp again, knowing they'd had a relationship in the past, twisted inside Ava like a knife. It hurt to let him go the other night. She knew if his plan was to move out to L.A. then letting go was the best thing to do to protect her heart, but that didn't make it any easier.

As her eyes moved from Jameson to the woman at his side, Ava wondered if Ms. Kemp knew of his plans to move to the West Coast. Perhaps she even had a home there.

Ava turned back to the microphone as the applause died down. "I want to thank each and every one of you for coming out tonight and supporting this cause. It's one that's dear to my heart, as some of you know. I've been handed the total figures for tonight." She unfolded the piece of paper. "With ticket sales, sponsors, the silent auction items and our bachelor auction, along with the donations we've collected tonight…" She glanced down at the amount. "Oh my. We surpassed our goal by over $100,000. For a grand total of $487,000."

There was a roar of applause.

She turned toward the curtain, where Stephanie stood just out of sight. "I'd like to bring out my sister, Stephanie, if I could."

Steffy moved to stand beside her, and Ava put her arm around her. "Without her help, this wouldn't be possible." She turned and addressed Stephanie. "I couldn't have done this without you, Steffy. You've worked tirelessly all year on this event, and you've been my rock for longer than you know." She turned back to the crowd. "Many of you may not know, but our sister, Lily suffered from this disease. She was struck with it at the age of fifteen and fought a good fight; unfortunately a cure didn't come quickly enough to save her. She died at the age of seventeen.

"It was always her dream to study music. And so, in honor of her, tonight I'm establishing the Lily Hightower Music Scholarship."

There was another round of applause. Ava turned and hugged Stephanie, who was near tears.

***

As the Gala winded down, Ava made her way

through the crowd, thanking sponsors and attendees as she went. Eventually, she noticed Jameson standing with Courtney Kemp. Lifting her chin and determined to handle the situation with dignity and class, she moved to thank the couple.

Jameson had a drink in his hand and took a sip, watching her approach. Ava pasted a bright smile on her face. She extended her hand. "Good evening, Ms. Kemp. It was so nice of you to attend, and thank you for the generous donation. It is greatly appreciated."

"You're very welcome. I could hardly let our boy, here, go for anything less than a show-stopping amount, now could I?"

Ava smiled over at Jameson. "No, of course not. And thank you so much for participating, Jameson."

He nodded. "It's a worthy cause, as you said."

"Thank you."

Looks were exchanged between them. Meaningful looks.

Courtney touched his arm. "I see an old friend across the room. I'll be right back, darling."

"Of course, Courtney. Go ahead."

Ava watched her walk away, wondering if the woman had caught the vibe between the two of them and was graciously giving them a few moments. For whatever reason, it left her and Jameson alone and gave her an opportunity to say what she felt needed saying. "So, I understand you're leaving."

"Leaving?"

"Yes, Jameson. Leaving town." She hoped he wasn't going to stoop to play games with her now, pretending like he didn't know what she was referring to.

"Who told you that?"

"I spoke with Ms. Thompson at your book signing. She told me she was there to lock up the deal for another season of *Inked Up*. In L.A. this time around."

Jameson nodded. "I see."

"So you're leaving?"

"What difference does it make to you? I'm only a means to an end for you, right? You just needed someone to headline your show."

She lifted her chin. "I suppose you're right, at that. If you'll excuse me, I need to say goodbye to the mayor."

He raised his glass. "By all means, can't keep the mayor waiting, now can we?"

She refused to be baited by his smart-ass remark, and took her leave. If he wanted to play the dick, he could go right ahead. She, on the other hand, would maintain a modicum of decorum and graciousness.

A few minutes later, out of the corner of her eye, she saw Jameson making his way to the exit, the lovely Ms. Kemp on his arm. A deep sadness welled up in Ava, overflowing as her eyes pooled with tears. She quickly made her way to the ladies room and wept in privacy.

CHAPTER THIRTY

Ava showed up at Brothers Ink on Monday morning. She nervously clutched the handles of her handbag as she waited while Max called up to Jameson's office and asked him to come down without telling him why.

Two minutes later, Jameson stopped short when he walked up front and saw her standing there.

"What are you doing here?" he snapped.

She'd come to confess her feelings, having had the worst two nights of her life, imagining him with Courtney Kemp. "I thought we could talk."

"What do we have to talk about? Our deal's done. You got what you wanted, and I'll get my parking spots at Wednesday night's City Council meeting, right?"

When she didn't answer, so hurt by his tone she was momentarily speechless, he prodded, "Right?"

She nodded. "Of course. Your spots. What else could you be concerned with?"

She turned and stormed out, but not before hearing

him call after her, "What the hell is that supposed to mean?"

She didn't stop, and he didn't chase after her. What had she expected? Truly, did she think he'd tell her it was all a mistake? That she hadn't heard Ms. Thompson correctly? That they hadn't offered him a second season? That it wasn't to be filmed in L.A.? What they'd had obviously hadn't meant to him what it had to her. What an idiot she must be.

***

Jameson watched her storm out. He'd blown it. He knew it the moment he opened his stupid goddamned mouth.

"You're an idiot," Max confirmed for him.

He twisted and glared at him.

"Think he already realizes that, Bro," Liam answered Max with a teasing smile at Jameson from where he stood with his arms folded, leaning against the counter.

"Then you'd think he'd stop fucking himself over," Max added.

"You'd think," Liam wholeheartedly agreed.

"Shut the fuck up, both of you," Jameson snapped and stalked away. He needed to think.

***

JAMESON

Jameson stood at his office window the next night, one hand on the frame, the other holding a rocks glass with a shot of whiskey. He stared out at the street and the people passing by as if he'd find the answers to his problems out there. He knew he wouldn't. He glanced down at his glass, swirling the ice and Irish whiskey. He wouldn't find the answer at the bottom of the glass, either.

Everything was off... across the board. He missed Ava. He needed her here. The shop wasn't the same without her. And the funny thing was, he'd spent the last six weeks trying to run her off, and now that was the last thing he wanted.

He turned at the sound of Max's footsteps. Great, just what he needed. "I'm in a bad mood; don't make it worse."

He chuckled, plopping down in a chair. "What else is new?"

"Cut the bullshit, and tell me what you want."

"Came to see if you've come to your senses yet."

Jameson turned back to the window and downed what was left of his drink. His senses? If he had any sense, he'd go after her, because one thing he knew for sure, no matter what happened between them, he couldn't return to the closed-off man he was before.

"Is it pride or fear that's stopping you?"

Jameson looked out the window. *Both*, he thought silently. And that was the rub of it. He wasn't a man to let anything keep him from what he wanted. He never let anything stand in his way. Now, for the first time in his life, he found it was himself that was standing in his own way. And why? Over silly bullshit.

Screw that. He looked over his shoulder at Max. "I've got an idea."

"This should be good," he answered sarcastically.

Jameson gave him an *I hate you* look. "If you want to see me make a fool of myself, come with me to the meeting tomorrow night."

Max grinned, reading his brother like a book. "You couldn't keep me away."

CHAPTER THIRTY-ONE

Ava sat at her place on the dais with the other council members. Her eyes ran over the agenda. It all seemed so insignificant. Everything that had once held importance in her life paled now that she knew Jameson would no longer be a part of it. She frowned. How had that happened so quickly? How had he gone from being the bane of her existence to being the meaning of her existence in just six short weeks? The worst part was in knowing she'd no longer even have the chance of catching a glimpse of him around town.

She wondered if his brothers would all go to L.A. with him. She supposed it would be an opportunity for all of them, especially Rory with his music. Hell, L.A. with its music scene, he'd probably never want to come back. What if that were the case with Jameson? Perhaps he'd love the West Coast, too. Maybe they'd close up their shop on Main Street and open up permanently in California.

The gavel pounded down, opening this month's session and drawing her attention from her dismal thoughts. She reached for her coffee, taking a sip. She hadn't been sleeping well and felt a deep depression settling over her. With the Gala over, she had little else to focus her attention on. Perhaps it was time for a change for her as well, but what? Pick up her business and move to another city? Start a new business, a new charity, a new hobby? Somehow now none of it seemed interesting or appealing, and she doubted it would fix her broken heart.

The meeting droned on, item by item, until finally they were drawing to the end of the agenda, the time when they would consider any new business the citizenry wanted to bring forward. She heard the doors in the back open, and she looked up. Jameson and his brothers strolled in.

Yes, they wanted their parking spots, of course. And she'd done her part. She'd spoken with all the members before the meeting, and told them how helpful he'd been with the charity. They'd readily agreed, like they probably would have months ago if she hadn't made such a fuss and turned their vote against him.

Now he stood there, waiting for his final part in

their deal. When the session concluded, and they opened the floor up for new business, Jameson approached the podium. "I'd like a moment of the council's time."

The presiding councilman leaned toward his microphone. "State your name, please."

With his eyes on Ava, he answered the man. "Jameson O'Rourke of Brothers Ink."

"State your business, Mr. O'Rourke."

"I'd like to propose the designation of the three parking spots in front of Brothers Ink be reserved for motorcycle parking. I believe the council will see that by doing so, we'll be able to keep one bike from taking up a standard size parking spot, and this way we'll be able to put three bikes in the same allotted space. Therefore freeing up more spots to cars and, in the long run, being a more efficient use of parking space."

"Motion to designate the three spaces in front of Brothers Ink on Main Street to motorcycle parking only."

"I second the motion," a member at the end said.

"All in favor say, aye."

"Aye," resounded throughout the dais.

"All opposed say, nay."

There was silence.

"The aye's have it. The motion is carried." The gavel slammed down.

"One more thing," Jameson spoke into the microphone.

"Yes, sir?"

"This is for councilwoman Hightower."

Ava was sure her face looked stricken as Jameson called all of her colleague's attention to her. She leaned toward her microphone. "Yes, Mr. O'Rourke?"

"I didn't know you. I judged you without knowing you. I based it all on you turning down those parking spots. I was wrong… about everything. But through it all, you stuck it out. You showed me that backbone, that spirit, that determination that has seen you through some hard times in your life, Ava. And I know your greatest fear in this life is failing. But you haven't failed, Ava. Not once. Not at anything you've ever done, despite what you think.

"But you've been wrong about a few things, sweetheart. I know you hate hearing that, but I'm going to point them out to you. You were wrong about me taking that job in L.A. You were wrong about what you think I find important. Hell, I'd wager to guess you were even wrong about me and Courtney Kemp."

A murmur went up in the room.

JAMESON

"Mr. O'Rourke, this is highly unusual," the presiding councilman said.

"Let him finish, please. I'd like to hear what he has to say," Ava said into her microphone.

"But most importantly, you were wrong about how I feel about you and what you mean to me. I'm in love with you, Ava. And I'm sticking around. So don't think you'll be able to get rid of me so easily, sweetheart."

He approached the dais. He stood before her, his hands in his pockets. "I'm standing here, babe, and I'm not going anywhere. And in case you missed that last part. I'll say it again. I'm in love with you. So, you got some smartass comment to say to that?"

She smiled down at him, her eyes welling with tears and shook her head.

"Then get your ass down here, woman."

She got up, ran around the bench, and flung herself at him, her arms wrapping around his neck. He lifted her off her feet as the entire chamber broke out in cheers and applause.

Jameson scooped her up in his arms and carried her out of the room like Zack Mayo carried Paula out of the paper bag factory in *An Officer and a Gentleman*.

In the back of the room, she saw Max, Liam, and Rory all standing and cheering, their ear-piercing whistles echoing loudly.

Jameson carried her down the hall and onto the elevator. When the doors slid shut, he set her down, holding her close.

"You sure about this?" she asked, staring up at him with a big grin.

"Never been more sure of anything in my life."

She lifted her chin. "I can be kind of a pain in the ass, I've been told."

He grinned. "I'm learning to live with it."

"Oh, are you?" Her brows rose.

"I've been told I'm a stubborn jerk," he admitted.

The corner of her mouth pulled up. "I'm learning to live with it."

"Good answer."

"We gonna make a go of this, Jameson?" she asked, all teasing aside.

He stared down at her with that confidence and determination she'd grown to love and found she couldn't live without, and he answered her. "You and I, what we feel? It's fundamental. It's like hunger, like breathing. I *need* you. And you need me, too. Fuck, yeah, we're gonna *make a go of it*, Ava, and it's gonna last a lifetime."

And that was all the assurance she'd ever need.

JAMESON

EPILOGUE

Ava —

I tilted my head back into the pillow, glancing above the bed at the frame on the wall, mounted dead center above the headboard. Jameson, who lay naked on top of me, nuzzled my neck, his mouth pressing kisses along my skin.

"I can't believe you framed that," I said.

He lifted his head and followed my gaze. Then a big grin broke out across his face. "Hey, that's to remind you what a hot commodity I am. I did go for ten grand, remember?"

I stared up at the Gala flyer that had carried his name and photo, proclaiming him the headlining bachelor. "How could I ever forget?"

He chuckled, and I felt the rumble of his laughter through his chest. "Babe, if it wasn't for that flyer, would we be here right now?"

I glanced around the room — his bedroom at the farm... correction, *our* bedroom. He'd moved me in not long after the city council meeting that was still the talk of the town six months later.

"That framed flyer is staying right where it is," he decreed, then continued kissing his way down my neck and across my chest. "To remind me every day what a lucky man I am." His mouth trailed lower across my belly—a belly that even now was growing with my little baby bump. "You hear that, little one? Daddy's a very lucky man."

I threaded my fingers through his hair. I was happy he thought so, but I knew the truth. *I* was the lucky one, and I didn't need anything to remind me of that fact.

Jameson picked that moment to blow a raspberry on my belly. Then he looked up at me grinning.

I giggled. Yep, I was one lucky woman.

THE END

Preview of MAXWELL

Brothers Ink

Maxwell was bent over the arm of a client, twisting and leaning to get to a difficult area of shoulder when the bell over the front door tinkled, drawing his eyes up for one brief glance. He saw the back of someone in a hooded rain jacket as they turned to close the door. The sound of the pouring rain traveled through the shop, along with a cool mist that blew in.

His eyes flicked to the clock; it was lunchtime, and they'd called their order in to Thai Garden two blocks away. He hoped this was the delivery boy with their food.

His eyes again flicked to the entrance, and then did a double take as the hood of the raincoat was pushed back.

Holy hotness.

She was a petite Asian beauty with long silky hair and big dark eyes. Not too much eye makeup, just thick dark lashes and a bit of liner. Her skin was flawless. She stepped toward the far wall, her eyes up on the framed art, and her body came into view from around the reception counter. The rain slicker hung open in front revealing a slender, boyish frame. Low slung jeans hugged her hips and exposed a teasing inch of skin between them and her tight top. Nice rack.

Clicking off his machine, his eyes returned to the client in his chair. "Give me just a minute, Ryan."

"Sure, no problem. I could use a few minutes break, anyway."

Max smiled at the man and got up to greet their new customer. He moved to the lobby and around the front of the reception counter, leaning an elbow on it. His eyes swept over the young woman, again falling to that gap between her jeans and top. Her belly was flat and toned, and her skin looked like silk. He hoped she wanted some ink; he'd love to work on her.

His gaze followed hers as she leaned closer, examining the art and photographs of tattoos the shop had done, her eyes moving all over the colors on the wall.

"See anything you like?" he asked. When she didn't respond, he spoke a little louder. "Miss, anything I can help you with?"

Then his eyes dropped to the bag that hung by her side and at the same time the aroma of the best Thai food in town found him. It was their lunch order. His eyes moved back up to her face. She wasn't the skinny Asian kid who usually delivered their food. Kiet was his name; they knew him well, as they ordered so often. But in all that time, this girl had never delivered their food.

"How much do we owe you?" he asked. She still didn't answer, so he stepped closer to her and repeated it a little louder. "Miss, how much for the food?"

Just then she turned and took a step, bumping right into his muscled chest. Her eyes got big as she stared up at him, taking a step back, obviously startled by his presence so close to her. He reached out a hand to steady her, but she flinched back as if she were afraid of him. He was a big man with muscled arms covered in tribal ink, and he knew that could be intimidating, especially to a petite girl like her.

He smiled, hoping to put her at ease and put his hands up. "Sorry. I'm Max. You're not the usual kid that delivers our food. I think his name is Kiet. Do you know him?"

She stared at him, but didn't answer, and Max wondered if she didn't speak English. She held out the food to him and pointed to the receipt stapled to the bag. He reached out and took it, smiling, hoping to reassure her. His eyes moved over her face. Her beauty took his breath. How was a girl this beautiful reduced to running food deliveries?

He twisted to set the bag on the counter, checking the receipt for the amount, and then he dug his wallet out. As he thumbed through for the money, he twisted, calling over his shoulder, "Liam, you got a ten? I'm short."

When he turned back, he noticed the girl's attention had returned to the art on the walls.

"Do you like our art?" he asked.

Liam walked over, handing him a ten, and they both studied the woman as she stared at the wall.

"Maybe she doesn't speak English," Liam murmured.

"Damn, right about now, I wish I spoke Thai," Max whispered back, and Liam grinned at him. Max reached to grab the bag and hand it to Liam to take to the break room, and his elbow knocked a glass candy bowl to the floor. It shattered with a loud crash.

"Shit," Max jumped back. As he looked down at the broken glass, he felt an elbow in his ribs and glanced up to find Liam nodding toward the girl. Max's eyes swung to her and noticed she hadn't even turned at the loud noise.

"I think she can't hear, Bro," Liam whispered.

Max took the ten from Liam, added it to his own, and tapped the girl on the shoulder.

She whirled, startled.

He held the bills out to her, nodding toward them.

Just then, Liam made some gestures with his hands. Max frowned, watching him. "When the hell did you learn sign language?"

The girl looked relieved and gestured back, a big smile breaking across her face, as she was able to communicate. They continued signing back and forth.

"What is she saying?" Max asked.

"Says her name is Malee. Kiet is her brother. He's sick and couldn't make the delivery, so her father sent her."

Liam signed some more, gesturing to the wall. She signed back, a shy smile on her face. "She likes the colors."

He signed some more. She signed back.

"She likes to draw. The art fascinates her."

Max watched her closely.

"Can you read lips?" Liam asked her, and she waggled her hand, and then gestured. "Says she tries, but she still has trouble with it."

Max gestured up to the art on the wall and spoke

clearly to her so she could read his lips. "You want a tattoo?"

Her eyes got big, and she pointed to herself.

He nodded.

She shook her head.

Max ignored the broken glass, too consumed with speaking to this beautiful girl. "Ask her if I make her nervous?"

Liam signed to her, laughing and making symbols that had Max thinking his brother was calling him a big gorilla. The girl giggled and blushed, and then she shrugged and held up two fingers about an inch apart.

He smiled, understanding that sign and asked, "Why?"

She made a motion with her hands, like she was trying to wrap them around a large bowl, and then pointed to his bicep. "Big," she tried to say the word that seemed foreign to her mouth.

He took her hand gently in his and brought it to his muscle revealed by his short-sleeved shirt. He smiled as her eyes got huge as she touched his skin, almost as if she'd never touched a man before, and suddenly she pulled back, embarrassed, and he was left wondering if she really hadn't ever touched a man.

Then suddenly, she backed up a step. She dipped

her head down, her eyes looking up from under her brow. Then she turned and dashed out of the shop.

Max followed to the window, watching her hurry down the street. "She was beautiful, wasn't she?"

Rory walked up taking in the glass on the floor and Max staring out the window, and then turned to Liam. "What's he looking at?"

Liam grinned huge. "Big brother is in love."

"Say what?"

"I just saw it happen, right before my eyes. He fell hard."

Max swiveled his head back. "She's pretty is all I said. Don't make a thing out of it."

"Yeah, right. Why do I suddenly feel like there's a lot of Thai food in our future?"

Max shoved his shoulder as he walked past him toward the back. "Speaking of, clean up the glass and maybe I'll let you have some of it."

"Me? I didn't break the damn bowl, you did!"

Max laughed and kept walking.

***

Malee turned and glanced back at the tattoo shop, studying the name. *Brothers Ink*. She'd never been there before. She'd lied to the man when she'd said her brother was sick and her father had sent her. Her father rarely let her out of the restaurant, preferring to keep her back in the kitchen, like her deafness somehow made her flawed and should to be hidden away. Her mother said he was just being protective of her, but sometimes she wondered if he wasn't ashamed of her disability. She wasn't perfect like her brother, who could do no wrong in their father's eyes.

She glanced back at the shop. She wasn't supposed to make that lunch delivery. She'd grabbed it and run out the door while her brother was busy, glad to escape the confines of the restaurant, even if it was only for a few minutes. Her father may beat her for her disobedience when she returned, but it had been worth it. She'd never seen art like that before. All the colors and designs had taken her breath away. She'd been fascinated. Tonight, in her room, she'd pull out her hidden sketchpad and colored pencils and try to duplicate the beautiful designs.

Her mind turned from the art she'd seen in the shop, to the big man who'd spoken to her. Max, he'd said his name was. Tonight, when she was alone in her room, in addition to her drawing, she'd also practice saying his name out loud until she got it just right, so if she ever got the chance to run into him again, she could say hello to him, and he wouldn't think she sounded funny.

She knew her lack of hearing distorted her voice, but it was hard to form the words correctly when you couldn't hear how they came out.

Her mother wanted her to get an implant that the doctor said would help her to hear, but her father forbid it, saying it was too risky and too expensive.

Her eyes again strayed to the tattoo shop as she stood on the corner in the rain, waiting for the light to change. She'd seen that man before. She'd seen him in the gym on Fourth Street where her brother took martial arts classes. MMA, they called it—Mixed Martial Arts. She'd seen Max in there working out on the bag. He had powerful arms, and she'd been mesmerized watching him. She wasn't supposed to go there either, but sometimes she snuck down there when her brother went and watched through the big storefront windows. No one ever noticed her. She made sure to stand off to the side, trying to be as inconspicuous as possible.

And now she knew where the big man with the powerful arms worked. Brothers Ink. She smiled a secret smile as she jogged back toward her parents' restaurant, happy for the first time in a long time.

END OF SAMPLE

Also by Nicole James
Find these on Nicole's Website: nicolejames.net

The Evil Dead MC Series

OUTLAW

CRASH

SHADES

WOLF

GHOST

RUBY FALLS